THE THINGS OWEN WROTE

The Things Owen Wrote

JESSICA SCOTT KERRIN

GROUNDWOOD BOOKS
HOUSE OF ANANSI PRESS
TORONTO BERKELEY

Published in Canada and the USA in 2017 by Groundwood Books

Permission to reproduce the poem "Gestur" on page 154 has been granted by Ivadell Sigurdson, wife of the late Paul Sigurdson.
Stephansson, Stephan G., "Gestur" (1909), in *Stephan G. Stephansson, Selected translations from Andvökur*. Translated by Paul Sigurdson, 34–6. Edmonton: Stephan G. Stephansson Homestead Restoration Committee, 1987.
The poem excerpted on page 163 was included on a display panel in The Stephansson Study at the Icelandic Emigration Center in Hofsós, Iceland.

Groundwood Books / House of Anansi Press
groundwoodbooks.com

We acknowledge for their financial support of our publishing program the Canada Council for the Arts, the Ontario Arts Council and the Government of Canada.

Canada Council   Conseil des Arts
for the Arts   du Canada

ONTARIO ARTS COUNCIL
CONSEIL DES ARTS DE L'ONTARIO
an Ontario government agency
un organisme du gouvernement de l'Ontario

With the participation of the Government of Canada
Avec la participation du gouvernement du Canada | Canadä

Library and Archives Canada Cataloguing in Publication
Kerrin, Jessica Scott, author
The things Owen wrote / Jessica Scott Kerrin.
Issued in print and electronic formats.
ISBN 978-1-77306-029-3 (hardcover).—ISBN 978-1-77306-030-9 (HTML).—
ISBN 978-1-77306-031-6 (Kindle)
    I. Title.
PS8621.E77T45 2017   jC813'.6   C2017-900655-X C2017-900656-8

Jacket design by Michael Solomon
Jacket art by Christiane Engel / Good Illustration Ltd

Groundwood Books is committed to protecting our natural environment. As part of our efforts, the interior of this book is printed on paper that contains 100% post-consumer recycled fibers, is acid-free and is processed chlorine-free.

Printed and bound in Canada

MIX
Paper from
responsible sources
FSC® C016245

For Peter and Elliott who traveled all the way
around the Ring Road with me.

Það er rúsínan í pylsuendanum.

ONE

Another casserole has been left on Owen Sharpe's front porch. This one is in a dish with a school of fish printed in turquoise around the middle. Its loose-fitting glass lid is all steamed up. The casserole is warm and smells faintly of cheese, onions and beef.

"Pops!" Owen calls out after he eases past the screen door, bringing the casserole inside with both hands. The door slams shut with a bang behind him, yet nobody yells at Owen about the jarring noise. He smiles to himself because of the relaxed house rules. Then he hollers, "Where's all this food coming from?"

Silence.

But Owen knows that his granddad is there somewhere. Neville Sharpe has moved in to take care of Owen while his parents are in Las Vegas, celebrating their anniversary.

"Pops!"

"In the kitchen!" his granddad calls back.

Owen steps over the tossed and abandoned shoes that have piled up this past week and heads to the kitchen. His granddad is sitting at the table, which is covered with cardboard filing boxes. There are even more on the floor.

"What's all this?" Owen asks while sliding the warm casserole onto the stovetop.

Owen's granddad flips the lid off one of them and peers inside. He scratches his head, leaving his feather-white hair sticking up at the back. His black-framed glasses rest heavily on his long, pointed nose.

"This is Gunnar's life's work," Neville says with a grand sweep of his hand.

"Who's Gunnar?" Owen asks.

"My friend Gunnar. Or, I should say, my late friend Gunnar. You probably don't remember him. He died a few years ago."

"Why do you have his boxes?"

"His wife has decided to sell her house and move to Edmonton to be closer to her son. She asked me if I could sort through Gunnar's office and see if any documents should be donated to the archive he worked closely with in northern Iceland."

"What's so special about Gunnar's stuff?"

"He translated Icelandic poems and stories into English," Neville explains. "He was even recognized for his work by the Icelandic government. They gave him a medal, which I'm sure to come across in one of these boxes."

"Hey, I know of an Icelandic poet. He moved to Alberta as a homesteader," Owen recalls. "His name was Stephansson."

"Stephan G. Stephansson. How do you know about him?"

"My grade-seven field trip last year. We visited his historic house."

"That's right. Stephansson House. Near Markerville. I haven't been there in years."

"I took some photos. Want to see?"

"Sure," Neville says, sitting back in his chair.

Owen's granddad gave Owen a camera for his last birthday. Owen has been taking photographs of practically everything ever since.

He drops his knapsack to the floor and roots inside it for his camera. He clicks through the files until he finds what he is searching for. His granddad leans in to watch on the screen.

Owen lands on Stephansson's little pink house, which is pretty with its green gingerbread trim. Owen took the shot at a rakish angle, a simple photographer's trick to make something look more dramatic than it really is.

"I remember it now," Neville says.

He continues to look at Owen's photographs, now of the inside of the house: the woodstove in the kitchen, the dining table set with china dishes, the butter churn, the upright piano, the spinning wheel. Owen clicks through to Stephansson's study, the room where the poet would write at his homemade desk. There was also a cabinet filled with Icelandic books and a horsehair-stuffed sofa to lie down on and think.

Owen keeps clicking through his tour at an even pace until he comes to a photograph of a bat. Its tiny body is wedged into the flowery wallpapered corner of Stephansson's dining room, near the plaster ceiling.

"Is that a bat?" Neville asks, peering closer.

"Neat, huh?" Owen says. "The guide told us that the attic is full of them. Hundreds of them, maybe. They fly out in a great big cloud every night to hunt for bugs, then return in the morning. This one probably left from the attic the wrong way and got trapped inside the house."

"I didn't think a bat could get confused like that."

"Oh, sure," Owen says. "The guide told us that it can happen whenever a shaft of light from inside the house shines into wherever the bat is roosting. It tricks the bat into thinking that the light marks the way to go outdoors."

"What happened to the bat?" Neville asks.

Owen shrugs.

"Maybe the guide turned out all the lights and opened the door at dusk so that the bat could find its way home," Neville suggests.

"Maybe," Owen says.

He is not sure why his granddad cares so much about one confused bat.

Neville takes his glasses off and cleans them with a cloth from his pocket. He puts his glasses back on.

"Let's see more pictures of the historic site," Neville says.

Owen clicks through more photographs, only now each one features the bat. Just the bat.

Bat.

Bat.

Bat.

Then selfies with the bat.

Then photographs of his best friend, Kevin, posing near the bat.

"Looks like you boys got distracted," Neville says drily.

Owen grins as he leans back in his chair. When he does, he spots dirty plates that have been stacked from breakfast along with three empty casserole dishes in mismatched patterns on the counter.

"Seriously, Pops. Who is sending all these casseroles?"

"It's the ladies from the Red Deer River Readers Book Club," Neville says.

Owen's granddad gets up from the table and digs out a fork from the cutlery drawer. He lifts the steamed glass lid from the dish on the stovetop and pokes at the warm contents.

"Ah. This is Pauline's work," he muses. "An abundance of mushrooms."

Owen gets up to have a look.

"You like mushrooms?" he asks. He hates them.

"Not particularly," Neville says, frowning.

"I don't get it," Owen says. "Why is she making you food? And why so many mushrooms?"

"I guess she forgot that I don't like them, but she's well-meaning," Neville says. "They all are. Pauline. Jóhanna. Marjorie."

"The ladies from the Red Deer River Readers Book Club?" Owen guesses.

"Yes."

"Don't they think you can cook?"

His granddad shrugs.

"Because I've seen you cook. You've cooked plenty. Especially since Grandma died."

Heavy silence.

Oops. Owen wishes he had not said that last part. It has been over a year since his grandmother, Aileen Sharpe, passed away, but still.

Neville stares at Owen, a boy with a nose like his own and gray eyes that are spaced widely on his freckled face.

Owen stares back. Whenever he is unsure, his left eye is slower to blink than the right. He is blinking like that now, which makes him look like an owl.

His granddad pats Owen's shoulder, then returns to the table and starts sorting through a new box.

Glad that the awkward moment has passed, Owen glances out the kitchen window. Beyond the backyard shed and the solid wooden fence that separates the Sharpes' garden from the neighbors, the endlessly flat prairies roll under a giant blue sky.

Owen returns to the table. He's got nothing better to do. There hasn't been any homework this past week because it's near the end of the school year. All his classes have been reviews so that students like Kevin can catch up before exams. Owen is an A student, so he can afford to coast.

"Have you found anything for the archive?" Owen asks.

"Yes, indeed," Neville says as he rummages through piles of documents on the table. "Have a look at this."

Owen's granddad plucks a small narrow notebook from the jumbled mess. Part of its marbled blue cover is worn right down to the cardboard beneath, and its loose binding is barely holding the pages together. He hands it to Owen as if he is handing him a little baby bird.

Taking his granddad's cue, Owen opens the notebook carefully. The water-stained pages contain lines of cursive writing in delicate spidery penmanship.

"This was the travel journal that Stephansson kept as he crossed the ocean during his emigration from Iceland to North America. You can see how he's teaching himself a new language," Neville explains.

Inside are lists of words that Stephansson translated from Icelandic to English.

Boat words.

Weather words.

Farm words.

"Gunnar tracked down this journal as part of his translation work. I'm sure that the archive in Iceland would dearly love to have it."

Owen's granddad rummages some more and comes up with a modern-day notebook like the kind Owen uses at school. He hands it to Owen, who begins to flip through the pages.

"That's Gunnar's notebook about Stephansson's travel journal. He writes about how he came across it. I thought I'd send it to the archive along with Stephansson's journal. The two seem to go hand in hand."

Gunnar's notebook is mostly in English, but he has cramped chicken-scratch writing, which Owen finds difficult to read. Plus, there are no sketches or drawings to make the notes interesting. He hands the notebook back to his granddad, who places it with Stephansson's travel journal off to the side.

"I didn't just take photos of Stephansson House. I also took notes during our field trip," Owen recalls, "along with some sketches."

"Really? Can I see them?" Neville asks.

Owen goes to his bedroom and pulls open his desk drawer. He finds his field notes among his other grade-seven notebooks, which are stacked on top of his grade-six ones and so on all the way down to his earliest efforts, a perfect record.

After returning to the kitchen table, Owen opens his field notes and scans the first page. It starts with a list of facts that the costumed guide told them about Stephansson: when he was born, when he emigrated from Iceland, when he moved to Alberta to start a farm. Owen keeps scanning, then selects an excerpt to read out loud to his granddad.

"Look here. It's about the color pink. 'During restoration of the house, some of Stephansson's descendants thought that the heritage people got the color wrong, but the heritage people did tests on paint chips from the house and proved that pink was the color back in 1927, the year that Stephansson died.'"

His granddad nods along.

Owen flips the page and studies the sketch he completed of the floor plan for Stephansson's house, a house that was built in stages over many years as Stephansson's family grew. He turns the notebook around so that his granddad can better see the sketch.

"Nicely done," Neville says, adjusting his glasses.

Owen reads another excerpt out loud. "'Stephansson couldn't sleep. He farmed in the day and wrote his poems all night long.'"

"An insomniac. I forgot about that," Neville says. "I wonder if he knew about drinking warm milk. That always does the trick for me."

At the mention of milk, Owen realizes that he is thirsty. He gets up and goes to the fridge. He reaches for the chocolate milk. He shakes the container and discovers that it has just enough.

When Owen's granddad sees what Owen is doing, he goes to open the cupboard to retrieve a glass. Only he sets down a coffee mug in front of Owen instead.

Owen holds the milk carton uncertainly.

"That's for coffee, Pops," he says.

Owen knows what to use. Why doesn't his granddad?

Owen blinks, owl-like.

His granddad clears his throat.

"I know that. I'm getting *myself* some coffee."

He strides to the counter and makes a big show of pouring a cup from a pot of coffee that sits on the stove.

"Now, let's hear more from your notes," he says as he sits down at the kitchen table.

Owen takes one sidestep over to the stove. He lifts the coffeepot. It is stone cold.

"Do you want me to heat that up for you?" Owen asks delicately.

"I like it cold," Neville declares, but he winces after he takes a sip.

Owen shrugs, then finishes off the milk carton by drinking directly from its spout. Wiping his mouth with the back of his hand, he returns to the table and reads out loud from the next page in his field notes.

"'Stephansson was possibly one of the best Canadian poets who ever lived.'"

"Gunnar told me that, as well," Neville says. "But not too many Canadians know about Stephansson because he wrote everything in Icelandic. That's why Gunnar's translations are so important. He had Icelandic roots himself and Stephansson was one of his favorite poets."

Owen's granddad grows quiet. He takes a sip of his cold coffee, winces again and puts the mug down.

"I'm hungry," he says. "Let's call it a day. I'll go through the final boxes in the morning."

But Owen is no longer listening. He has flipped ahead in his notebook and now pauses. He remembers all the poetry assignments that followed his class trip and he also remembers why he doesn't want anyone to see his work, especially his granddad.

Owen's cheeks flame red.

As soon as his granddad gets up and goes to the sink to dump his cold coffee, Owen quickly closes his notebook and shoves it underneath some of Gunnar's paperwork strewn on the table.

"How about you get us some plates," Neville says.

Owen gets up on shaky legs to fetch some dishes from the cupboard. His pounding heart slows down as his granddad scoops casserole onto their plates.

When they sit down at the table, Owen's granddad pauses with his fork halfway to his mouth.

"Gunnar wanted your grandmother and me to visit Iceland. When he passed away, his wife gave us a travel voucher for two free tickets to go there, which is what Gunnar had written in his will."

"You didn't go?"

"No. That was right about the time your grandmother got sick. She couldn't travel because of her treatments, but she would have liked to. The Icelandic landscape is supposed to be spectacular."

"I've been photographing landscapes around here," Owen says, picking out the mushrooms and moving them to the side of his plate. "I submitted some to the yearbook committee today."

"What of?" Neville asks.

"Prairie things. You know. Water towers. Hay bales. Combines."

"I'm sure one of your photos will get picked for the cover," Neville says confidently.

Owen grins. He can always count on his family to say something along those lines.

When they finish eating, they get up to rinse their plates. Owen notices that only his plate has a pile of rejected mushrooms. His granddad's plate is scraped clean.

"I thought you didn't like mushrooms," Owen teases.

"Who told you that?" Neville asks.

"You did," Owen says.

"No, I didn't. I love mushrooms."

Owen hesitates. His granddad ate all the mushrooms, so maybe he does love them. Perhaps Owen misunderstood earlier, and Pauline from the Red Deer River Readers Book Club got it right after all.

Owen tries to let the confusing moment go. It's only mushrooms, he reasons, as he scrapes the uneaten ones from his plate into the compost. Still, his doubt niggles at him for the rest of the evening. Even when he goes to bed, there's no escape. He dreams about the poor befuddled bat at Stephansson House, and forgets about his notebook hidden on the kitchen table that he wants no one to read.

TWO

The next day when Owen arrives home from school, another warm casserole is on the front porch, this one in a polka-dot dish.

"Pops!" Owen calls out after he eases past the screen door, carrying the casserole inside with both hands once again. The door bangs shut with a satisfyingly loud *whump*. There are even more tossed shoes piled up at the door, and they are becoming a challenge to step over.

"In the kitchen," his granddad calls.

When Owen walks in, he sees that Neville is starting to put documents back into Gunnar's boxes and stacking them against the wall.

"Did you find anything else?" Owen asks after depositing the latest casserole onto the stovetop.

"Nothing more. I couriered Stephansson's travel journal and Gunnar's notebook to the Icelandic archive this morning. But I also came across this. Have a look."

He holds out a tiny box in his palm. Owen takes it and removes the lid. Inside is a medal that is cradled in silk.

The medal is shaped like a knight's white cross with a blue oval disk in the middle. On that disk is a golden bird standing with its wings outstretched as if about to take flight. The medal is topped with a clasp that looks like a royal crown.

"That's Gunnar's Order of the Falcon," Neville explains. "It's a medal from the Icelandic government that he received for translating Stephansson's poems. Gunnar was so proud of receiving it, and rightly so. He brought it up every chance he got."

Owen plucks the medal from the box. It is much heavier than he expects.

"Wow. This looks like something that a king would wear," Owen says. He carefully puts the medal back inside the box and hands it to his granddad.

Owen remembers something else that the costumed guide from his field trip to Stephansson House told the class.

"Stephansson's wife was given a medal, too, after Stephansson died, along with a fancy Icelandic dress. The dress was on display, but her medal wasn't," Owen recalls.

"No? Why not?" Neville asks.

"The guide told us that when someone who has been given the medal dies, it's supposed to be returned to Iceland," Owen says.

"Returned? Are you sure?"

"Pretty sure."

"Can you double-check your field notes?" Neville asks.

Owen's notebook! His thoughts go jagged. Why did he mention something else he knew about Stephansson?

Owen reluctantly gets up to retrieve the notebook from his bedroom, but then he remembers that he hid it on the kitchen table yesterday beneath some of Gunnar's papers.

"I left it here," Owen mutters, sitting back down.

He roots through the piles of documents that his granddad hasn't yet put back into boxes. Only, he can't find his notebook.

His granddad starts to help.

"What color is it, again?" Neville asks.

"Green," Owen says, not looking up from his search.

"You mean yellow," Neville says. "Here it is."

Owen's granddad passes him a yellow notebook. Owen has a quick glance and shakes his head.

"That's not mine. Mine's green."

"No, Gunnar's was green. This is yours."

Owen's granddad continues to hold out the yellow notebook.

Owen grabs it, opens the cover and points to the author's name written in chicken scratch.

"No. See? This is Gunnar's. Here's his name."

Owen tosses the notebook aside and continues his frenzied hunt. He doesn't want his granddad to find his notes before he does.

"Oh," Neville says in a soft voice.

Owen pauses. He looks up.

"What?" he asks, thinking his granddad has found his notebook and opened it.

His granddad says nothing, but he is still holding Gunnar's notebook. He flattens down the hair at the back of his head with a shaky hand.

A freight train whistles forcefully in the distance. Owen's granddad doesn't flinch — the sound is so familiar.

But the enormity of what his granddad might have done hits Owen as shockingly as if the freight train has derailed and slammed through the walls into their kitchen.

"Pops. Did you send the wrong notebook?"

"I suppose I did," Neville says, staring at Gunnar's notebook as if it had somehow tricked him.

Owen can barely swallow. His notebook! The things he wrote! Oh, no!

"Where? Where did you send it?"

"To the archive in northern Iceland. By courier. It will arrive this weekend."

His granddad plucks a tattered road map of Iceland from the table and unfolds it. He shows Owen precisely where his notebook is headed. The map is covered in Gunnar's handwritten notes about historic sites to see, all related to Stephansson.

Owen's mouth goes dry, dry as a dust cloud on the prairies after weeks of no rain. On top of that, he knows he's doing his owl-blinking thing.

"It's no big deal," Neville reasons. "I'm sure the archivist will love to read your field notes about Stephansson House. After all, he's one of their most beloved poets. I'll courier Gunnar's notes tomorrow, along with my letter about the mix-up, and the archive will mail yours back."

Owen tries to think. Sure, the archivist might enjoy what Owen wrote, but Owen knows for certain that his granddad would not. And that's going to be a huge problem because the archivist will use his granddad's return address on the envelope. Owen's notebook will be delivered straight into his granddad's hands!

Owen can't let that happen.

He just can't.

But how can he stop it?

"So, Gunnar's medal," Owen says hesitantly, a desperate half-baked plan forming in his mind. "Don't you think we should return it?"

"Return it? To Iceland?"

Owen isn't sure where Iceland is. Somewhere up north, he thinks. The name is a dead giveaway. Still, there is no room for Owen to falter.

"Absolutely," Owen says. "That's what the guide at Stephansson House told us."

Owen's granddad slowly leans back in his chair to consider.

"I suppose that I can courier it like I did with Stephansson's travel journal and your notebook," he says.

Alarm bells go off in Owen's head.

"No, Pops! Bad idea. Gunnar wanted you to *see* Iceland. You said so yourself. You told me that he even gave you two free tickets. So I'm thinking that we could go this weekend. You and me. We could return the medal ourselves, drop off Gunnar's notes at the archive and — oh, hey — I could get my notebook back. Easy peasy."

Owen is trying hard to make his voice sound light and breezy. Normal. He knows he isn't telling the full truth of the matter, but the thought that his granddad might discover the things Owen wrote is too much to bear.

Owen's granddad studies Owen as if he is actually thinking about his crazy suggestion.

"We'd have to check with your parents," Neville says, more to himself than to Owen.

"Yes, sure, let's do that."

"Do you have a passport?"

Owen marvels that he's able to leap another barrier.

"Yes! Mom and Dad got me one when they got theirs to go to Las Vegas."

"Where is it?" Neville asks.

"My desk," Owen says triumphantly.

"I suppose we'd only be gone for a few days," Neville muses out loud.

Owen's thoughts race as he tries to come up with more selling points. What can he remember about Iceland from the field trip to Stephansson House? He knows that the Vikings settled there.

He knows that there might be falcons flying about because of Gunnar's medal. What else? If Iceland is up north, there must be lots of ice.

"I know where my winter coat is," Owen says. "So packing will be easy."

"Oh, you won't need that. It won't be cold. It's June, same as here. But in Iceland, there'll be close to twenty-four hours of sunlight."

"The sun doesn't go down?"

"Barely at this time of year," Neville says. "Iceland's up near the Arctic Circle. Still, there won't be as much ice as you might think."

"Good," Owen says, thinking that this must be a plus.

"What you're more likely to see are geysers."

"What are geysers?"

"Geysers are vents in the ground that hurl boiling water from deep inside the earth high up into the air. Iceland also has volcanoes."

"Do they still erupt?" Owen asks, thinking that this is another plus.

"On occasion. But mostly there are vast lava fields from former eruptions. Gunnar told me that the interior parts of Iceland are so rugged, astronauts trained there to prepare them for landing on the moon," Neville says.

That's enough pluses, Owen thinks. He takes a deep, steadying breath.

"So, we can go? To return the medal?" he asks, hoping against hope.

To Owen's great relief, Neville slowly nods yes.

Owen jumps up before his granddad can change his mind.

"Great! Let's get packing!"

"Right," Neville says. "I'll go home to find that travel voucher and I'll call your mom and dad from there. You stay here and pack a suitcase. Don't forget your passport."

Owen doesn't have to be asked twice. He bolts from the kitchen and makes a dash for his parents' bedroom where they store the suitcases. He hears his granddad shut the front door, putting their plan into motion.

Owen rushes to the closet. He flings open the doors. Dresses. Pants. Housecoats. Suit jackets. Above that, boxes of toys that Owen has outgrown, all neatly labeled, as well as his dad's long-abandoned rolled-up yoga mat. Below the hanging clothes, on the floor, are several overcrowded shoe racks along with more abandoned exercise gear. But in the far corner of the closet on his dad's side, Owen spots the small suitcase he is looking for.

Owen pulls it out and hauls the suitcase to his bedroom. He makes a beeline for his dresser but wonders what to bring. He has never had to pack by himself before, so he is unsure. He yanks open a drawer and pulls out a few balls of socks. He piles them on the bed.

Underwear. He will want some, so he opens another drawer and pulls out a few pairs to add to the pile.

What else? Jeans besides the pair he is wearing? Yes, and an extra T-shirt, too. Owen finds his favorite, the one his cousin made for him that reads *Failure is not an exit strategy.*

What about a sweater in case he gets cold? He hears his mom's voice in his head, but he realizes that a sweater would not be a bad idea, so he pulls out a turtleneck and lays it on the bed with the rest of the items.

Bathroom stuff, he thinks. He is particularly proud of himself as he scoops his toothbrush, paste and comb from his cabinet. But he passes on the dental floss like he does every night, unless he is forced to use it. He hates flossing.

Owen returns to his bedroom. He piles his things into the suitcase. At the last minute, he remembers that they will be staying overnight, maybe even two nights. He returns to his dresser and finds a fresh pair of pajamas to toss in, the blue-and-brown flannel ones with the rodeo theme that he has slightly outgrown. He zips up his suitcase just as the front door opens.

"Owen!" Neville calls.

Owen bolts to the front door. His granddad has combed his hair nicely, he's wearing a tie, and he's pulling a small rolling suitcase with one hand and carrying his old briefcase from when he used to work for the government in his other hand.

"Your parents are fine and I've cashed in the travel voucher with Icelandair," Neville says. "They offer a direct flight from Edmonton. We'll leave tonight. If we can get on the road within an hour, we'll make it to the airport in time."

"Great!" Owen says.

He is going to Iceland! He really is! He'll have his notebook back in no time, and no one will be the wiser.

They step over the tossed-shoes pile and go straight to the kitchen.

"Where's your suitcase?" Neville asks.

"All packed," Owen reports. "I'll go get it."

When Owen returns to his bedroom, he is pretty confident that he has packed everything he needs. He half expects that his granddad will ask to inspect his luggage, but when he doesn't, Owen feels proud. He deposits his suitcase at the front door on his way back to the kitchen.

"And your passport?"

"Oops," Owen says sheepishly.

"Don't worry. There's a lot to remember," Neville says.

Owen returns to his bedroom and pulls out his passport from the desk drawer. He dutifully hands it over to his granddad. His granddad slides it into his briefcase for safekeeping along with Gunnar's yellow notebook and his map of Iceland.

"We should eat before we head out," Neville says.

He takes the lid off the warm casserole on the stovetop. But then he does something strange. He opens the cupboard and sets the steamed-up lid on top of the stack of clean plates. Without a word, he shuts the cupboard.

Owl-like, Owen stares at his granddad.

"What?" Neville asks when he sees Owen staring at him.

"I … I'll get us some clean plates," Owen offers.

Owen goes to the same cupboard, removes the casserole lid from the stack of plates and sets it next to the sink, all the while eyeing his granddad, who is now peering into the casserole dish. Owen lays out two clean dishes.

There *are* a lot of travel details to remember, Owen reasons. No wonder his granddad is a little absentminded.

They sit down to eat, and Owen is delighted to discover that today's casserole doesn't have mushrooms.

"We're really going to Iceland," Owens states before his first mouthful. He is checking to be absolutely sure.

"Yes, but don't forget," Neville says. "We're there on serious business. We're going to return Gunnar's medal."

"And switch the notebooks," Owen adds.

"That's right," Neville says. He checks his watch. "We better hurry," he says, and he digs into his food.

They eat in silence, lost in their own thoughts about their upcoming mission.

After they get up to rinse their plates, they put everything, including all the empty casserole dishes and their lids, into the dishwasher and store the extra food in the fridge.

"Remind me to call the ladies from the Red Deer River Readers Book Club when we get to the airport. I need to put a halt to their casserole deliveries. I don't want good food going to waste while we're away," Neville says.

"Will do," Owen says, but he is only half listening because he is rooting through a kitchen drawer to find extra batteries for his camera.

Owen's granddad grabs his car keys.

"Wagons, ho!" he announces.

THREE

Owen's granddad locks the front door, and together they load their luggage into the trunk of his car. They get in and buckle up. Neville backs out of the wide driveway and they hit the highway. They are making good time.

Owen sits back to enjoy the drive. They will head from Red Deer to the Edmonton airport, passing farmers' fields, tractors moving between young rows of crops, and the occasional oil drill pumping up and down. Every patch of land is surrounded by cattle fences or a hedgerow to slow down the persistent prairie wind. There is a wide divide between their three lanes of heavy traffic and the three lanes going the other way between Edmonton and Calgary, two rival cities on the flat Alberta plains. The scenery spreads endlessly beneath an enormous blue sky unmarked by a single cloud.

Fields.

Fields.

Farm buildings.

Fields.

Fields.

Tractor.

Every now and then, there is a tight cluster of trees standing alone in an empty pasture. Owen remembers what his granddad once told him. Whenever there is a clump of trees like that, it probably marks the ruins of an old farm, but the house and the people who planted the trees around the homestead are long gone.

Owen pulls out his camera and takes a few photographs of the wide-open scenes as they fly by, while his granddad plays his favorite radio station, CBC. When the interviewer asks a question, sometimes his granddad answers back. But mostly he concentrates on the road and the large number of transport trucks zooming past filled with supplies or live cattle, everyone except them driving well over the speed limit.

After they see the Edmonton airport up ahead, Owen's granddad takes the turnoff and expertly parks the car in the crowded lot. They retrieve their luggage and walk through the main entrance for Departures. They check themselves in at the kiosk and make their way through the security gate.

"It's a good thing we have carry-on bags," Neville says. "It makes things easier."

They are now in the waiting area, listening for their airplane to start boarding.

"I left a message at your school and told them that you'll be away tomorrow," Neville says.

"Good thinking," Owen says, having forgotten that tomorrow is Friday, a school day.

Then he remembers that he made plans with Kevin for that weekend. They were going to bike along the trail beside the Red Deer River and then cut across to the skateboard park where they would watch a regional skateboarding competition.

"Can I borrow your cell phone, Pops? I need to call Kevin to tell him I won't be home this weekend."

His granddad hands him the cell phone. Owen dials the number. Kevin answers.

"Kevin? It's Owen. Listen. I can't go biking this weekend."

"Oh? Why not?" Kevin asks.

"I'm going to Iceland."

"Yeah, sure you are."

"I am. I'm at the Edmonton airport right now."

"But your parents are in Las Vegas, aren't they?"

"I'm here with my granddad. He has two free tickets to Iceland and he needs to return his friend Gunnar's medal."

Owen leaves out the whole notebook-switching fiasco. Even his best friend doesn't know about the things Owen wrote in his field notes.

"Medal? What medal?" Kevin asks.

"A medal for translating poems. Stephansson's poems."

"Stephansson? Isn't he that guy with the house full of bats?"

"Yeah. That's him."

"And you're at the airport?"

"Yeah."

"Are you kidding me?"

"No. Listen." Owen holds the cell phone up so that the overhead speakers can be heard announcing their flight. "See?" Owen says.

"Really? You're actually going to Iceland?"

"Yes."

"Awesome!"

"I know! See you!"

Owen hands the cell phone back to his granddad. They line up to board the airplane. They show their passports and paperwork to the flight attendant, and she points out where they will be sitting.

Neville gives Owen the window seat, and Owen enjoys the roar of the takeoff. He looks down at the patchwork of land that they are flying over. It reminds him of the earth-tone quilt that his mom bought for his bed from the annual Agriculture and Craft Fall Fair. The ruler-straight gray highways and winding indigo-blue rivers thread through the patches like embroidery.

Owen's granddad explains that the view will soon change. Their flight will take them north. They will fly over the top part of Saskatchewan, across Nunavut, over the Northwest Passage, Baffin Island, Greenland and the North Atlantic Ocean to a city called Reykjavík in Iceland.

"Much of the view will be barren," Neville says. "Or the ocean. Not much to see."

"How long is this flight?" Owen asks.

"About six and a half hours," Neville says. "But remember, there's a time-zone difference. We'll be landing in the morning, only it will feel like the middle of the night to us because Iceland is six hours ahead of Alberta."

Owen nods. He doesn't really understand the time math, but he trusts his granddad's calculations.

Owen pulls a magazine about Iceland from the flap in front of his seat and starts to leaf through it. He pauses to look at the rugged landscape photographs. He studies the emerald-green, jet-black and pumpkin-orange lava fields. He reads about the most famous volcano in Iceland, Mount Hekla. He lets out a whistle when he sees the soaring flames and plume of smoke. He can practically feel the heat, the awe, the terror.

His granddad barely notices because he is buried in a mystery novel about a missing dog. He is using his favorite bookmark, the laminated bank receipt for the last paycheck he deposited before retiring.

Owen recalls that he drew an exploding volcano in his field notes when he learned that Stephansson's family had left Iceland following an eruption that poisoned the land.

His notebook!

A fresh wave of panic hits Owen when he thinks about what his notes contain, but then he quickly assures himself that he'll have them back soon enough.

The flight attendants come around with the meals, so Owen stows the magazine and pulls his tray table down. He chooses beef, which the attendant hands to him. So does his granddad, but the attendant has run out of beef. She apologizes and offers what's left: fish.

Owen wishes that his granddad did not have to order fish. He does not like the smell. It reminds him of the food flakes he used to feed to Fiona.

Fiona was his pet goldfish.

Was.

The memories flood back.

The day Owen brought Fiona home was so happy. He was shopping with his grandmother for a new bicycle helmet when they came upon the pet store.

"Let's go in!" Owen begged.

"Your parents are going to kill me," Aileen joked, allowing Owen to tow her inside despite her half-hearted protests.

As it turned out, the store manager was offering a special promotion to help celebrate the one-year anniversary of the store opening. She was giving out a free goldfish and coupons for goldfish flakes to anyone who would buy a bowl to keep the gold-fish in.

Owen could not resist. He picked out the one that had the purest shade of orange, and he called her Fiona because that was the prettiest name he knew. His grandmother even bought a castle for her bowl. When he got home, he set Fiona on a shelf above the kitchen sink where she could watch him from her world as he did homework at the table.

Owen was vigilant about not overfeeding Fiona, and he kept her water crystal clear. Whenever they went to Grande Prairie to stay with relatives for Thanksgiving or some other family event, Owen would arrange for Kevin to come in and take care of her.

"Don't overfeed Fiona," he warned Kevin repeatedly.

And just to be sure, Owen left his best friend with detailed instructions, which Kevin dutifully followed to the letter.

Fiona kept Owen company for years.

Then came the terrible period when Owen's grandmother became ill. Everyone spent more and more time at the hospital. Gradually, Owen did less and less homework. That meant he spent less and less time in the kitchen. When his grandmother finally slipped into a deep sleep, Owen and his family stayed at her side until the very end.

The days after coming home from the hospital were the worst. Everyone moved so quietly, so wordlessly. The air was so empty. It was hard to breathe. Weeks passed after the funeral before Owen's family could begin to move back into their routines.

One day, when Owen returned home from school, he looked up from his math equations to check on Fiona.

Only, Fiona wasn't there. Her shelf was empty.

Owen dropped his pencil. He couldn't remember the last time he had seen her.

He couldn't remember the last time he had fed her.

Or changed her water.

"Mom!" he cried out. "Mom!"

But then he remembered that his mom was running errands.

Owen frantically scanned the kitchen: the counters, the top of the fridge, the pantry. He bolted from room to room in a desperate search.

"Fiona! Fiona!"

Nothing.

Owen stopped to gulp deep, steadying breaths.

Gutted, he returned to the empty kitchen.

He slowly opened the doors to the cupboard beneath the sink where they kept empty glass vases.

His heart fell to his feet.

There was Fiona's bowl.

Clean and empty.

He knew then that he had failed Fiona, failed her terribly.

He knew his parents had been unable to bring themselves to tell him.

Owen sat down on the cold tile floor and wept.

Eventually, he dragged himself up, and with a shovel he found in the garden shed, dug a deep hole in the flowerbed along the fence and buried her bowl. Just before he covered it, he dropped a large stone on top, smashing the bowl to bits.

No goldfish would ever replace Fiona.

Owen made certain of that.

"How's your dinner?" Owen's granddad asks.

Owen is picking away at it, so lost in his thoughts about Fiona. But his granddad jolts him back into the airplane, and Owen dutifully scoops up a mouthful.

"Pretty good," he says between bites.

And it is. No mushrooms.

After the flight attendants return to collect the empty trays, everyone on the airplane pulls down their window shades and settles in to sleep. Even the overhead lights on the airplane are dimmed so that only soft pastel patterns appear on the ceiling, mimicking the northern lights. The flight attendants quietly disappear into the back of the airplane.

"You best get some shut-eye," Neville says, reclining his seat and bunching up a pillow against his head. He folds his glasses into his shirt pocket.

"I'm not really tired," Owen admits, but he obediently pulls down his window shade like everyone else.

"You will be when we land," Neville warns. He puts on his eye mask, leans his head against his pillow and doesn't say another word.

Owen cannot sleep knowing they'll soon be in Iceland. His thoughts race. He lifts the shade and looks out the window. It is still light out, but there is nothing to see because their airplane is flying above soft pink clouds. He looks away from the window and sees a passenger in the row beside their seats glaring at him because of the light coming into the cabin. Owen sheepishly shuts the shade. He digs out his camera and clicks through the photographs of his field trip to Stephansson House. He slows down when he comes to the ones of the poet's front porch with its green gingerbread trim.

He pauses to study a close-up. Then he notices something above the top window dormer. It is a wooden cutout of a crescent moon, painted green like the rest of the decorative trim.

Owen zooms in on the green moon with his camera. It reminds him of a favorite bedtime story that his grandmother used to read to him when he was very small, something about saying good night to the moon and other things in a great green room.

A familiar dull ache blooms in his chest.

Owen glances at his granddad to see if he can read Owen's thoughts, but his granddad looks asleep.

When she was alive, Owen's grandmother invited him to stay over whenever he wanted to. They had a spare bedroom on the third floor, the attic, of their house. It had sloped walls and windows at each end. The room was painted green, just like in the story she liked to read to him.

But she had just as many stories of her own to tell. The story about her honeymoon was one of Owen's favorites. He can almost hear her voice now.

"We went to Ontario, to an area called Thousand Islands. It is a sightseer's paradise. Public lighthouses, fairy-tale castles, maritime museums, quaint little waterside towns with darling boutiques. Your granddad had it in his head that he wanted to rent a sailboat named *Little Fish* for a few days," Aileen told Owen.

"Well, I went along with it, only I didn't know how to sail and I had no interest in learning. But I decided that I could be happy just to sit and relax. After all, this was your granddad's vacation, too. So I put on my big sun hat, grabbed my book and tucked myself into the corner of the cockpit with my iced tea. Still, he kept trying to get me involved, barking out orders like Captain Bligh. 'Trim the sail! Pull in the sheet! Drop the anchor!' And all I wanted to do was read my novel!

"Then he got mad at me. 'Look,' your granddad said. 'You need to learn how to sail this boat. What if I fell overboard?' And then I got mad and said, 'I don't want to learn, so you best not fall in!'

"The next thing I know, your granddad drops the sails, takes off his shoes and then jumps — that's right — *jumps* overboard. As he treads water, the boat I'm in drifts, and he calls out, 'Turn the engine on, then come around and get me.'

"I couldn't believe it. Talk about stubborn! Who is this person I married? So, I calmly put down my book, went below, found my life jacket and put it on. Then I came back up into the cockpit and jumped overboard myself. Without another word, I started swimming to shore so that he had no choice but to catch up to the boat, climb on board and steer it away from the rocks."

"I guess that taught him," Owen always said.

"It most certainly did," Aileen always replied. "And that's why we're so happily married."

To this day, Owen wonders who was the more stubborn of the two given that both of them ended up in the water, fully clothed, with their boat drifting away.

Owen stows his camera and sits back in his seat. He looks over at his granddad, who is snoring soundly, mouth slightly open, eye mask askew.

The airplane starts to bank east over the vast steel-gray North Atlantic Ocean. Somewhere up ahead, Iceland beckons.

But back at home, a lady from the Red Deer River Readers Book Club is leafing through her favorite cookbook, searching for a tasty casserole recipe to make and drop off on Owen's front porch where no one is home.

FOUR

The Alberta prairie sun inches across the inside of the blue bowl sky. Below it, Marge Figgis has just come back from Tasty Foods, Red Deer's discount grocery store. She is unloading the ingredients for a new casserole recipe onto her spotless kitchen counter.

"How was the car?" Hardy Figgis bellows from somewhere in the basement where he is tinkering.

"It's still making that noise," Marge yells back at her husband.

It's been making that noise for weeks.

Hardy mutters in reply, but he is too far away for Marge to make out his words. She could walk over to the top of the stairs and ask him to repeat whatever he said, but that would take her away from her task at hand, which is to make a casserole for Neville Sharpe and his grandson, Owen.

Today is Friday. It is her turn.

Marge digs out her *Five Roses* cookbook with its battered and butter-stained cover and turns to page 264. She scans the instructions for Beef and Barley Casserole. She is not a particularly good cook, so she has to follow the recipe to the letter.

Marge washes her hands at the sink and ties a clean linen apron around her plump waist. She turns on her kitchen radio for company.

CBC.

Marge fills a pot with water, adds salt and turns the stove on to High. When the water boils, she adds the barley and sets the timer for twenty minutes, which is what the recipe tells her to do. At exactly twenty minutes, she turns the stove off.

Meanwhile, Hardy climbs the basement stairs to see what she is up to. He is always checking on her. She does not check on him nearly as much, but he is so busy checking on her that he does not notice.

He turns down the radio, which annoys Marge.

"I'm making a casserole for Neville Sharpe," she announces before he even has a chance to ask.

She knows Hardy that well. They have been married for forty-seven years.

Hardy consults the calendar posted on the fridge.

"It's not your turn. It's Jóhanna's turn according to the almighty fridge calendar."

Hardy hates the fridge calendar because it tells him everything that needs to be done on a daily basis: a lifetime of chores.

"I know," Marge says. "But I have some ground beef that I need to use up, and Neville is taking care of his grandson, Owen, this week. Growing boys eat a lot, so Jóhanna dropped off something for lunch and I'm covering dinner."

Hardy walks to where she is standing to read the recipe over her shoulder.

"'Beef and Barley Casserole,'" he reads out loud.

He pulls a face behind her back. He has had casseroles too many times to count and he does not like them. He finds them too bland and the leftovers go on for days. He is surprised to see that this recipe calls for chili powder.

"Are you really going to add the chili powder when you make this?" he asks.

"Yes," Marge says hotly. "I'll put in what it calls for. A quarter of a teaspoon."

"Well, triple it," Hardy suggests.

"I most certainly will not *triple* the chili powder," Marge declares. "I'll do exactly what it calls for. You're a maniac."

Hardy huffs. He goes to the kitchen's back door and begins to take it off its hinges.

Marge barely glances from her work. Hardy is about to perform a familiar task: the shaving of a door.

Their old house is unique. It slants — not by much — to the right. It is as if their house is shouldering the constant prairie wind. And being slightly slanted is hard on rectangular doors. Every so often, they get stuck. When that happens, Hardy takes the door down and shaves a bit of wood off the top or the bottom with his hand planer so that it fits better. Over time, all the doors of their house have taken on a slightly trapezoid shape.

"Is your book club this afternoon?" Hardy asks as he works on the door.

Marge is a member of their neighborhood's monthly book club called the Red Deer River Readers. She hates the club very much. She thinks the other members pick trashy books that have too much senseless violence or kissing scenes. Who wants to talk about violence or kissing at a book club?

Not Marge, that's for sure.

There is a book right now on her night table that is only half-read and badly written. Even the cover is embarrassing — two people groping at each other in front of a stone castle that's on fire — so she keeps it facedown.

Still, Marge faithfully attends all the meetings, which are now held at Neville Sharpe's home. She is convinced that if she does not go, the group will talk about *her*, and she hates that idea even more than being forced to read books she would never pick for herself. To cope, she brings her knitting to block out their endless chatter.

The only one who liked the book club even less than Marge was Aileen Sharpe, Neville's wife.

Marge smiles to herself.

Aileen Sharpe.

What an opinionated crank.

No one could get a word in edgewise or dared to disagree with Aileen if she was in the room.

But deep down, everyone had to admit that Aileen was always right. And whenever Aileen got fed up with the club's latest book choice, she would insist on a novel that was difficult but entirely unforgettable. Members of the club might not have liked Aileen, but they certainly respected her and they read anything she recommended from cover to cover.

Aileen was smart. She made the best rhubarb crisp in town. She would do anything for her grandson, Owen, whom she bragged about constantly.

And until she was struck down by cancer a little over a year ago, she jogged every day in her bright red runners, even in the rain.

Marge misses Aileen very much. The whole book club does. When Aileen got sick, the club started meeting in her living room where she would lie in the orange recliner. It was her chair.

Before she died, Aileen made the club promise that they would continue to meet at her house, and she left them with a reading list to keep them busy for years. What she was really asking them to do was look out for Neville. Neville now lets them come and go as they please.

Occasionally, someone at a club meeting will bring up Aileen's funeral and the poem that Owen wrote and read during the service. It moved everyone to tears, including Marge, who told Owen so at the reception right after the service. Upon hearing how she felt, he fled from the room. To this day, she still feels bad that she upset Owen when she only meant to be kind.

Marge pulls out a frying pan, gives it a dollop of corn oil and sautés the celery, green pepper and onions. A nice homey smell fills the air. She turns up the radio.

The kitchen door is fixed now, and Hardy has returned to the basement to retrieve his oil can. He comes back up and puts a few drops on the hinges of the back door he has just hand-planed.

"Is anything else squeaking?" he asks after turning down the radio.

"Not that I'm aware of," Marge says.

She grits her teeth, straining to hear CBC.

Hardy heads out of the kitchen to parts unknown.

Marge turns up the radio. She pulls out a baking dish and scoops the sautéed vegetables into it. She browns the ground beef in the frying pan, overcooking it to be safe, and adds the meat to the vegetables. Then she adds the canned tomatoes, barley and spices, including the chili powder, which she measures precisely. She sprinkles the grated cheese and breadcrumbs on top. She slides the casserole into the oven and sets the timer.

Marge goes into the living room with its bold sunflower-patterned curtains, plucks her knitting from the basket beside her chair and sits down to do a few rows while she waits. As she settles in, she thinks about the most recent conversation she had with Neville, just before he moved into his son's house to take care of Owen.

Neville was in the backyard repairing his fence when Marge arrived a week ago with a warm casserole — this one pork, beans and sausage.

"You ladies don't need to keep sending over casseroles," Neville told her. He had his tool belt on. "Really, I'm grateful, but I can manage."

Neville says this each time a casserole appears, but he eats them all the same.

"Of course you can," Marge replied as she always did. "Shall I put this in your oven to keep it warm?"

"Yes, please."

Marge ducked inside. She was not snooping — she never did that — but she had a quick look around after she slid the casserole into the oven and turned it on Low.

Nothing was amiss in the house. Sure, it could have been tidier. There were magazines and paperwork strewn on tables and empty coffee mugs scattered about. The vacuum stood in the corner at the ready, but Marge was pretty sure that it hadn't moved since her last visit. Still, the house was in good shape.

But something made Marge pause in the living room. It was the orange recliner, Aileen's orange recliner. Marge crossed the room and picked up a photo album that was lying on it. She was about to flip through the pages when Neville quietly entered the room.

"Is that yours?" he asked.

Marge felt sheepish. Her cheeks burned bright red.

"I'm so sorry, Neville," she sputtered, caught in the act. "It's so unusual to see anything on Aileen's chair. I didn't mean to pry."

"*Whose* chair?"

"Aileen's."

Neville looked at her for a long minute.

"Who's Aileen?" he finally asked.

Marge opened her mouth to speak, but no words came out. What did he mean, who's Aileen? Was he joking?

"Is that yours?" he repeated, pointing to the album she held awkwardly.

"Of course not. Why do you keep asking?" Marge said, her confusion mixed with growing alarm.

"I'm asking because I don't recognize anyone in those photos," Neville said matter-of-factly.

Marge sat down on the sofa and opened the album. It was full of photographs of a younger Neville and a younger Aileen. They were on picnics, on a sailboat, at county fairs, at the hot springs in Banff, at the Calgary Stampede — all happy moments early in their marriage.

"Neville," Marge said. "These photos are of you. You and Aileen."

Neville said nothing.

"Aileen," Marge prompted. "Your wife."

"I'm married?" Neville asked.

"You *were* married. To Aileen."

Silence pressed against the four walls of the room. Neville gave a small nod and sat down.

"How about a nice cup of tea? I'll go fetch us some," Marge suggested.

She didn't wait for an answer. Instead, she bolted to the kitchen and tried not to cry. Jóhanna and Pauline had been reporting Neville's odd behavior for months, and she had seen some things, too, but not like this.

Marge placed the teapot and two blue china cups on a tray after she pulled herself together and brought the tray into the living room. Neville had been flipping through the photo album. As soon as he saw her come in, he shoved the album aside.

"I could use a cup of tea," he announced brightly.

He seemed more himself. The cloudy air had lifted.

They sipped their tea for a bit, sitting next to each other on the sofa.

"What is wrong with the fence?" Marge asked, making small talk.

"I need to replace a few rotten boards," Neville

said. "I've been thinking about getting a dog."

"A dog?"

"Yes. For company," Neville said. "Maybe a little fox terrier. Or a sheepdog. I can't decide."

"A dog is a lot of work," Marge said. "You'd be forever vacuuming."

Marge glanced at the neglected vacuum standing in the corner behind Aileen's orange recliner.

"I know. I'm still weighing my options."

"What about your grandson? Doesn't he keep you company?"

"Owen's great company. But he's getting older. More independent. Creating his own life. You should see him with a camera." Neville sighed. "Anyway, I haven't decided about a dog. I know it would tie me down. I'm not sure I want to give up my freedom just yet."

"Yes, it's nice to be able to come and go as you please," Marge said.

"I used to travel a lot more," Neville admitted. "I miss it."

Neville grew quiet and Marge did not press further. When she finished her tea, she set her cup down on the tray and took Neville's cup when he was finished. She got up to do the dishes, and Neville followed her into the kitchen.

While at the sink, she said, "Pauline will be by tomorrow. She wants to try out a new chicken and broccoli recipe."

"Tell her I won't be here. I'm moving into my son's house while he and my daughter-in-law go to Las Vegas," Neville said, picking up a tea towel to dry the dishes.

"Then we'll drop off casseroles at your son's home," Marge said. "For you and Owen."

Marge's thoughts are interrupted by the buzz of the oven's timer. She sets her knitting aside and pulls the casserole out from the oven. It is oozing hot bubbling goodness. She wraps it up for transport in clean tea towels and calls down the basement stairs to Hardy.

"I'm leaving now!" she shouts.

Marge heads out the front door, carrying her warm casserole along with her knitting bag and half-read book. She climbs into their car. She drives down the wide suburban streets of Red Deer to Owen's home, which is six blocks away.

The car is making that noise again.

She pulls into the empty driveway. Neville's car is not there. This strikes her as peculiar. Neville is supposed to be minding Owen. She checks her watch. School is dismissed by now. Where is everyone?

Marge climbs out of her car and carries the casserole to the front porch.

Strange.

Another casserole is resting on one of the rocking chairs by the door. She recognizes the daisy-patterned dish. It's Jóhanna's. She touches the glass lid. The casserole is stone cold.

Marge stands uncertainly with her own warm casserole.

She scans up and down the street. A freight train whistles, and a lonely dog barks in the distance. On high alert, she hears both. Otherwise, all is quiet.

She hesitantly knocks on the door.

There is no answer, and now she is not expecting one.

She sets her casserole down next to the cold one and spies through the living room window. The lights and television are off, and everything appears to be in order.

She knocks again, knowing it is futile but not knowing what else to do.

Where are Neville and Owen? How long have they been gone for?

Marge gingerly tries the doorknob.

Locked.

Then Marge does something she is not at all comfortable doing. She lifts the lid of the wall-mounted mailbox next to the front door and peers inside, hoping she will not be caught snooping. She gasps. There is a handful of envelopes stashed in the box.

The daily mail has not been collected!

A wave of foreboding chills Marge. She backs away from the door, climbs down the porch stairs and scrambles into her car. She heads straight to the book club that is assembling at Neville's house for their monthly meeting. She is breathless, and her heart is racing. She almost misses a stop sign.

Calm down, she tells herself. Calm down. Deep breaths.

"You're late," Pauline announces loudly as soon as Marge rushes in. "Where's your book?"

Everyone is already seated in Neville's living room. It is a full house. Only Aileen's orange recliner is empty, since no one ever dares to take her spot.

"We're got more things to worry about than the whereabouts of my book. I've just been to Neville's grandson's house. Neville's not there," Marge reports.

Some club members close their books. Others stare.

"Perhaps he just stepped out," Jóhanna says. "On an errand."

"A pretty long errand," Marge says. "When did you drop off your casserole?"

"Just before lunch," Jóhanna says. "I left it on the porch. Why do you ask?"

"It's still there," Marge says.

Everyone who is wearing a watch now checks the time.

"Neville's been gone all day?" Jóhanna asks, alarm creeping into her voice

"Worse," Marge says. "I looked into the mailbox. Their mail hasn't been collected from yesterday."

"And there's no sign of Owen?" Jóhanna asks.

"No. Both are gone."

"But where? Today is a school day!"

Marge wraps her arms around herself and starts pacing.

"I …" She hesitates.

"What?" Pauline demands.

"I had a strange conversation with Neville when I dropped off a casserole last week."

"Strange? What do you mean?"

"He was looking at a photo album. He …" Marge gulps. "He couldn't remember Aileen."

Everyone glances at the orange recliner as if Aileen is still there and would be offended.

"Oh, dear," Pauline mutters.

"And then he talked about traveling. How he missed it. And how quickly Owen is growing up."

Marge shrugs. "I didn't think much about it at the time."

"Oh, no. You don't suppose ..." Jóhanna cuts in.

"I don't know what to think. It's just, they're not at home, and I'm sure they've been gone since some time yesterday."

Pauline stands.

"This is crazy. Let's just call Neville. Who's got his cell number?"

"No!" Jóhanna stands, too. "We can't call. He already suspects that we're on to him about his memory issues. You know how testy he gets. There's got to be another way to find out where he is."

Silence fills the room. Nobody moves.

"I've got it," Jóhanna says. "I'm going to call Kevin."

"Kevin?" Marge says. "That maniac skate-boarder?"

"Yes, that Kevin. He happens to take care of my cats when I'm away. He's also Owen's best friend. Maybe he knows something."

"That's brilliant," Pauline says. "Give him a call."

Jóhanna fishes out her cell phone from her giant purse. She consults the contact list and makes the call. She puts the cell on speakerphone as members of the Red Deer River Readers Book Club gather around her. A girl answers, Kevin's sister.

"Hi, Kayte. It's Jóhanna Porter. Is Kevin there?"

"Yes, I'll get him."

Marge starts to pace again.

"Hello?" Kevin says.

"Hello, Kevin. It's Jóhanna Porter."

"Oh, hi. Do you need me to take care of your cats?"

"No, it's not that. I am actually looking for your friend Owen."

"Owen? He's in Iceland."

"Pardon me?" Jóhanna manages to ask.

"Iceland," Kevin repeats matter-of-factly.

"That can't be right."

"I didn't believe him at first, either. But then I heard airport sounds when he called me on his granddad's cell."

"So he's with his granddad."

"Yes."

"Why would they want to go to Iceland?"

"Owen said that his granddad has to return a friend's medal."

"A friend's medal? *Gunnar's* medal?"

"Gunnar? Yes."

"Thank you, Kevin. You've been very helpful."

"Is Owen in trouble?"

"No, of course not. He's with his granddad, as you say."

Jóhanna mumbles goodbye and hangs up.

Everyone in the room knows about Gunnar and the Order of the Falcon. A conversation with him never went by without Gunnar mentioning his medal at least once.

"Well, that's it. We absolutely must call Neville," Pauline declares.

"He'll be furious with us," Jóhanna says. "He'll cut us off, and then we won't be able to look out for him like Aileen asked us to. He'll end up in a seniors' residence well before his time like my cousin Buddy Clark."

"No one's going to ship Neville to a seniors' residence! And anyway, there's Owen to consider."

"Neville wouldn't hurt him!"

"Not intentionally. But he's forgetful. His memory is getting worse."

Marge turns her back on the crowd and faces the silent and empty orange recliner, looking for the answer to an impossible question.

What would Aileen want them to do?

FIVE

A blue-uniformed flight attendant quietly makes her way up the darkened aisle, offering water to any passenger who is still awake. Owen opens his eyes and nods to tell her that he would like some. Moments later, he has to go to the washroom and regrets drinking the water. Now he either has to wake up his granddad to ask him to stand, or he has to crawl over him to get to the aisle.

Owen studies his granddad. He is still snoring, eye mask firmly in place.

Owen decides to crawl over him. At first, he manages okay, barely touching his granddad by precariously balancing on one leg and bracing himself on the backrest of the passenger's seat in front of him as he lifts his other leg over his granddad's lap. But Owen's legs are not quite long enough, and in the end he clumsily drags his other foot across his granddad's legs.

"What's going on?" Neville demands in a voice that is loud enough to wake up the passenger who glared at Owen earlier when Owen opened the window shade.

"It's just me, Pops," Owen whispers.

"What? Where am I?" Neville asks.

"On an airplane," Owen whispers.

"What? I can't see!"

"Take off your eye mask," Owen whispers.

"What eye mask?"

"Your eye mask," Owen whispers urgently. "You put it on to go to sleep."

Owen's granddad gropes his face and hauls off his eye mask. He blinks as he looks around, confused, his white hair sticking up at the back. He digs into his shirt pocket for his glasses and puts them on.

"Where are we going?" Neville asks again, his glasses crooked in his haste.

"Where are we going?" Owen repeats. "What do you mean? We're on our way to Iceland. Remember?"

But Owen's granddad continues to look baffled. Then he abruptly stands up to scan the airplane, front and back.

"Iceland?!" Neville repeats at a high volume. "That can't be right!"

Owen grows alarmed. Why is his granddad acting this way when he was the one with two free tickets to Iceland? Perhaps his granddad is not quite awake, Owen tries to reason. Perhaps he is still dreaming.

"Pops," Owen says gently, nudging his granddad's arm. "Wake up."

"Why is everyone asleep?" Neville asks loudly, yanking his arm away from Owen. Now Owen's granddad sounds frightened.

And that frightens Owen.

"It's nighttime," Owen says. "You should go back to sleep. I'm going to the washroom, and when I get back, I'll sleep, too, like you told me."

Owen's granddad does not sit down. He and Owen are the only ones standing on the entire airplane.

"Where are we going?" he demands again.

"Pops! Iceland!" Owen repeats, his voice straining.

Owen is now upset, but the other passengers around them are beginning to shift in their sleep, so he tries hard to remain calm. The passenger who had been glaring at him about the window shade is now looking on with pity. Owen can also see a flight attendant briskly making her way up the darkened aisle toward them.

"Can I help you?" she asks quietly but sternly, all business.

Owen answers to buy his granddad some time.

"I'm just going to the washroom," Owen explains. "I startled my granddad who was asleep." He turns to his granddad. "I'm sorry about that, Pops."

The flight attendant looks at Owen's granddad to confirm the story.

"Is everything okay?" she asks, softening her tone.

Owen's granddad glances at Owen and when he does, he looks like himself once again, focused and in control. He straightens his glasses and clears his throat.

"Certainly. I was sound asleep. Got a little confused, that's all. How much longer until we land?"

The flight attendant checks her watch.

"About four more hours," she says. "Can I get you anything?"

"I have a slight headache," Neville says while slowly sitting down. "Do you have any aspirin?"

"I'll check the galley," she offers kindly.

She returns to the back of the airplane and Owen follows her to where the washrooms are located. He ducks into one of them. When he is done, he steps out, only to find the flight attendant waiting for him. She smiles, but Owen remains wary. He peers down the aisle to make sure his granddad is still sitting where he belongs.

"How are you enjoying the flight?" she asks pleasantly.

"It's good," Owen says, keeping his answer short and safe.

"Have you been to Iceland before?" she asks.

"No," Owen says, shifting from one foot to the other.

"It's a beautiful country," the flight attendant says. "I love it. Especially the thermal springs."

"What are they?" Owen asks, intrigued despite his urge to return to his seat before anything else happens with his granddad.

"Iceland has these wonderful outdoor pools that are naturally heated by hot water from deep in the earth."

"Oh," Owen says, thinking he would like that.

"Are you traveling with your grandfather?"

"Pops? Yes."

"How nice. Is he okay now?" she asks.

Owen moves to high alert. Why is she asking? Are they in trouble? Is his granddad in trouble?

"Sure he is," Owen declares. "I startled him. That's all."

"And what brings you to Iceland?" she asks.

73

Owen immediately thinks about the mess with his notebook, but instead tells her the easier half-truth.

"My granddad wants to return a medal for a friend of his."

"Sounds like you're on an interesting mission. Well now, here are two aspirin. Would you please take them and this water to your grandfather?"

"Sure thing," Owen says, taking the pills and the bottle from her.

"Tell him I hope he's feeling better."

"Sure thing," Owen says again, relieved that she's letting him go.

He brings the medicine to his granddad, who gets up to let Owen back into his seat.

Suddenly, Owen *does* feel tired and maybe even a bit dizzy. He plumps up his airplane pillow, jams it against the cool window shade and closes his eyes. Hours later, he is awoken by the sound of the breakfast trolley rattling its way up the aisle.

Owen's granddad is already awake, watching the news on the screen in front of him with his headphones on. Owen taps his arm. His granddad removes his headphones.

"What time is it?" Owen asks. He is groggy and his mouth feels like cotton balls.

"Seven thirty," Neville says, checking his watch.

"But it will feel like one thirty in the morning to you. You're still on Alberta time."

Owen glances over at the grumpy passenger who is now awake and reading a newspaper, so Owen opens up his window shade. He squints. It is bright outside and he can see the steely ocean below, an endless field of rippling bluish-gray. He looks for boats. There aren't any.

The same flight attendant who helped them earlier with the aspirin reaches their aisle with her trolley. They eat their breakfasts. Owen particularly likes a white yogurt-type dish that is thick and wonderfully creamy, so he asks her what it is when she comes by with beverages.

"That's *skyr*, a famous Icelandic dish. It is a type of soft cheese."

"It's really good," Owen declares.

The next time the flight attendant walks by, she stops to slip him a second helping.

"Special delivery," she says. "And how's your headache, sir?" she asks Owen's granddad.

"Gone," Neville says. "Thanks for asking."

Owen's airplane flies over the tip of Iceland and he spots the outskirts of a small city from his window. There are rows of tiny square houses with colorful corrugated tin roofs.

Reykjavík.

The airplane banks, then lands on an airstrip surrounded by brownish-gray lava fields. There are no trees, but there are jet-black mountains looming in the distance, some even capped in snow. Owen also spots steam vents billowing white clouds from the ground. Geysers!

"*Góðan dag*. Welcome to Iceland," a flight attendant announces cheerfully over the intercom. "The local time is 9:15 a.m."

As soon as the cabin door has been opened, Owen takes a deep breath of the fresh air that rushes down the aisle.

"There's no smell!" Owen says, marveling that Icelandic air doesn't hint of wheat warmed by the sun, the smell he's grown up with.

They make their way out of the airplane, down the steps and outside across the tarmac. The sun is crisp and bright. They enter the airport. As soon as they are inside, they go through customs and show their paperwork. Then they walk into the main part of the terminal.

The airport is mostly glass with gleaming wood floors and clusters of metal seats in bright bold colors like the houses in Reykjavík that Owen spotted from the airplane. Huge screens hang down from the ceiling and are silently flashing all the flights of the day to European places that Owen has heard of at school or on the news.

Owen's granddad finds a banking machine and takes out money in Icelandic currency. It is colorful, like Canadian money. He slips some bills into his coat pocket but puts the rest into an envelope and hands it to Owen.

"It's good to keep money and important documents in several places when you're traveling. That way, if you lose something, you won't be completely stranded. Keep this safe in your knapsack."

Owen beams. He loves being treated like an adult. He tucks the envelope into an inside pocket next to his camera and zips everything up for good measure.

"We need to find a bus to get to the city. Reykjavík is about fifty kilometers away from the airport," Neville says.

As they stand in the bus line just outside the exit doors, Owen studies the people of Iceland, hoping to spot signs that they descend from Vikings. Then he realizes that he is being ridiculous. People in Alberta don't go around wearing cowboy hats. Why would people here wear helmets with horns?

A little girl breaks away from her family circle on the sidewalk near the airport doors and runs right up to Owen.

"*Halló*," she says, stopping short. She is wearing a bright hand-knit wool sweater that goes to her knees, and her almost-white hair is tied up in crooked pigtails.

That's the Icelandic word for *hello*, Owen thinks.

"Hello," Owen answers back.

"Where are you from?" she asks.

"Red Deer," Owen answers, impressed that she speaks English, too, although with an accent.

"Reindeer?" the little girl repeats. She giggles. "That's an animal."

"No, *Red* Deer. It's a place," Owen corrects. "In Canada," he adds.

"Canada," the little girl repeats. "Our reindeers are brown."

"So are ours," Owen says, and he realizes that he has no idea why his city is named Red Deer. "I'm Owen. What's your name?" he asks.

"Britta," she says.

Owen knows it is important to say something nice whenever he first meets someone, so he says politely, "I like your sweater."

Britta looks down at her hand-knit sweater as

if seeing it for the first time. She looks up at Owen and smiles again.

"Are you flying somewhere today?" Owen asks.

"No, my grandma is coming to take care of me while my mommy goes away."

"Oh. How long will your mom be gone for?"

"Seven sleeps," Britta says proudly.

Owen smiles. He used to count days by the number of sleeps when he was little, too.

"Britta," her mom calls while holding out her hand. "Let's go to Arrivals. Grandma's airplane has just landed."

"Bless, bless," Britta says to Owen, and she runs back to her family.

When the bus arrives, Owen and his granddad climb aboard and take a seat near the back.

The driver heads down the highway and follows the signs to Reykjavík, which are easy to spot. But there are other place-names, too. They are long and are made up of strange letters. Some have dots and squiggles on top or are smashed together in pairs. Owen tries to pronounce them as the signs whip by his window, but he cannot work his mouth fast enough. Outside, the dark brown lava fields endlessly roll by, all scabby with only pale moss and lichen for a thin cover. It is not much to look at, so Owen keeps his camera in his knapsack.

"What's the plan?" Owen asks his granddad.

"First off, we'll need to return Gunnar's medal," Neville announces. "The protocol office that handles them will be closed on the weekend."

"What day is it today?" Owen asks.

His thoughts are still fuzzy and he feels a bit crusty himself, like the lava field they are cutting through.

"Friday," Neville says.

"It doesn't feel like Friday," Owen says. He yawns.

"You're all messed up because of the time difference," Neville reminds him.

But even though he is tired, Owen hasn't forgotten his number-one priority.

"After we return the medal, then we'll go to the archive?" Owen asks.

"Yes. Only, the archive is on the northern coast of Iceland where Stephansson grew up," Neville says. "We'll need to rent a car, but the drive won't be too long. Iceland is a very small country."

They enter the city and slow down as they wind their way through the narrow streets of Reykjavík. The streets are sided with plain cement buildings that are jammed against each other like the unfamiliar letters that Owen spotted in the signs. The buildings are painted in soft yellows, blues, greens and reds. Everything looks so tidy: no litter, no graffiti, no billboards.

They stop at a traffic light near an old graveyard that is fronted by massive iron gates. Speared on top of the gateposts are assorted solo wool mittens looking for their lost mates after a long winter. The mittens are brightly knit like the sweater belonging to the little girl Owen just met. He digs out his camera and takes a photograph of the comical display.

At last, their bus pulls up to its station. The driver jumps out and helps passengers down with their luggage.

Owen's granddad flags a taxi driver and hands him an address. They climb into the backseat and take a short trip to where they will return the medal. The taxi pulls away, leaving them alone on the curb in front of a white mansion where the protocol office is located. Across the street is a park that features an enormous pond.

Owen pulls up the handle of his suitcase to start walking, but his granddad doesn't make a move.

"Aren't we going inside?" he asks.

"Sure. In a minute."

Still, his granddad doesn't budge.

"What's wrong?" Owens asks, searching his granddad's face for clues.

SIX

Owen and his granddad continue to stand on the sidewalk in front of the white mansion that houses the protocol office. Owen wonders if his granddad accidentally left his briefcase with Gunnar's medal in the taxi, but no. His granddad holds his brief-case firmly in his right hand, safe and sound. Then why don't they head straight to the protocol office to return the medal? Wasn't that the plan?

Owen shifts from one foot to the other. The sooner they return the medal, the sooner they can get on with retrieving his notebook, Owen thinks. Maybe if he starts walking toward the stone walk-way of the mansion that leads to the wooden front door with the massive iron knocker, his granddad will follow?

Owen takes a couple of tentative steps in that direction, pulling his suitcase along.

"I was thinking about Gunnar," Neville says, still not moving. "He was so proud of his medal. It was even on display at his funeral."

Owen turns to study his granddad. His clothing is wrinkled from the flight and there is a grayness under his eyes because of lack of sleep. His wispy white hair is sticking up at the back once again. But it is the way Owen's granddad remains rooted to the spot while thinking about the friend he has lost that makes Owen sad.

"Maybe we should sit for a minute," Owen suggests, setting aside his own worries for the time being.

Owen's granddad nods gratefully. They walk across the street and into the park. They sit down on the first empty bench they come to alongside the pond. People stride by, dressed for work, all business suits, skirts and messenger bags. The sky has clouded over, and the pond is now the color of dull gray putty.

"Can I see the medal one last time?" Owen asks.

His granddad digs out the little box from his briefcase. He passes it to Owen with hands that shake a bit.

Owen carefully lifts the shiny enamel cross from the box and holds it flat in his palm. It quickly warms in his hand.

"I'd like to earn a medal like this someday," Owen muses.

"I'm sure you will," Neville says without hesitation.

Owen continues to stare at the medal, mesmerized by its beauty.

"No," Owen says flatly. "Medals like this are for creative people. Writers. Poets. Musicians." Owen sighs. "I'm none of those."

"Why do you say that?" Neville asks, shocked.

Owen shrugs.

"You're creative. You're very creative."

Owen shakes his head.

"Well, I have a fridge at home plastered with your drawings that says otherwise."

"That's just little-kid stuff I drew with Grandma," Owen says.

"Okay, what about your photography? That's coming along nicely, isn't it? You even submitted some of your landscapes to your yearbook committee."

"Sure. I guess." Owen still isn't convinced.

"What about your work at school?"

"My schoolwork? That's not creative."

"I disagree! The sketch of Stephansson House you drew in your field notes was very well done."

Owen sits up quickly at the reminder of his notebook. He's done with this topic. He hands back the medal and the box to his granddad.

The sun pops out from behind a cloud and is warm on their faces. There are birds pecking at the ground nearby, but the little flock leaves Owen and his granddad alone, sensing that they don't have any breadcrumbs.

Owen's granddad is not done.

"And what about the poem you wrote about your grandmother for her funeral? Everyone was so moved," Neville says. "I still hear members of the Red Deer River Readers Book Club mentioning it from time to time."

Owen swallows hard but says nothing.

They sit for a bit, staring at the glass-smooth pond. Owen scoops up a pebble and tosses it in. A ripple carries toward the far side where there's a bench occupied by a very large man scratching at the neckline of his Nordic sweater, a price tag still attached to the sleeve. He sits beside a jogger who is wearing red runners. The shoes remind Owen of his grandmother, making him sad all over again.

Owen's granddad sighs. He holds the medal out and gently rubs his thumb over the enameled white cross. Then he places the medal to his chest over his heart. Owen knows to look away. His granddad puts the medal back in the box and carefully closes the lid.

"I think I'd like to do this next part on my own," Neville says somberly.

"Sure thing, Pops. I'll stay here with our luggage."

"I won't be long," Neville says as he reluctantly gets up.

Owen watches as his granddad makes his way across the street to the white mansion. He is moving slowly, the way he did at Owen's grandmother's funeral.

Owen sits back on the bench to wait. He digs out his camera from his knapsack and searches for the series of potential yearbook photographs that he took of the Alberta prairies: the water towers, hay bales and combines. He had been excited to submit them to the yearbook committee, but now he can see room for improvement. The sunlight falling onto the water towers could be more vivid. The hay bales could be more striking with a close-up shot. The combines could look more imposing if he had included the billowing clouds of dust behind them.

All Owen's life, he's been told how talented he is, how smart he is, no matter what he does. His dad pins his report cards to the bulletin board in his office. His mom brags endlessly to friends and family on the phone about his latest accomplishments such as his projects for the annual science fair or the cake he baked her for Mother's Day.

She told everyone that the cake was delicious, the best she'd ever had. But Owen knew that couldn't possibly be true. He put in too much salt, he overbaked it, and the icing turned out runny.

Owen loves everyone's praise, no question. He thrives on it. Still, he wonders if he sometimes coasts because no matter what he does, he can depend on his family to back him up.

Owen looks at his prairie photographs some more. He realizes that he should have stayed outdoors longer for the photo shoot. He might have had better results if he had truly pushed himself and taken artistic risks instead of going for easy praise and moving on to the next thing to tackle.

Now he thinks about Kevin. Kevin is not an A student. Sometimes he's not even a B student. Kevin is passionate about one thing: skateboarding. It's all he talks about, and he doesn't just talk. He practices every night for hours, he goes to training camps, and his bedroom walls are covered by posters of his skateboard heroes. Owen knows that Kevin will still go watch the regional skateboarding competition even without Owen this Saturday, because he would never miss an opportunity to learn from those athletes.

Kevin pushes himself to the limits. He makes many spectacular mistakes. But he's not afraid of failure.

Owen wonders what that would feel like.

It seems like a long time later, and Owen is about to get up and knock on the mansion's front door to look for his granddad, when Neville emerges. He crosses the street and walks toward Owen with a slight bounce in his step, as if a heavy weight has been lifted from his shoulders.

"All set?" he says to Owen.

"So they took back the medal?" Owen asks.

"Not at first. But luckily I remembered to bring a copy of Gunnar's obituary to back my claim."

Owen knows that an obituary is a published story about someone who has died. He keeps a copy of his grandmother's tucked into the last book she ever gave him, which was about a boy who loved rockets.

"Smart thinking," Owen says, impressed that his granddad thought of bringing the obituary, just in case. "So now we'll rent a car and head to the archive?"

"You bet," Neville says. "But first, I think we should grab something to eat before we find a car-rental agency."

Owen doesn't argue. He's hungry, too, he realizes.

They walk along the path beside the pond, towing their luggage until they reach the end and enter into the downtown streets of Reykjavík. They wheel their luggage inside the first café they come to.

It is warm and colorful. The walls are a buttery yellow with gold trim around the windows. The chairs are bright orange with black legs. The polished wood counter where they sit down is resting on bookshelves jammed with travel guides and atlases arranged by continent, and the ceiling is plastered with maps of the world from which orange lamps hang down to match the chairs. Ketchup bottles and salt and pepper shakers are grouped together and spaced regularly along the counter. Owen fiddles with the ones closest to him.

"What is a typical Icelandic breakfast?" Neville asks the server when he comes by to take their order.

"We're not known for lavish breakfasts. Mostly we look for something easy and piping hot to be scarfed down before braving whatever storm, volcanic eruption, earthquake or avalanche that might be waiting on our doorstep."

The server says this with a smile. He is used to tourists.

Owen's granddad laughs.

"I would recommend our *hafragrautur*, or oatmeal," the server suggests. "It's been a staple in the diet of Icelandic families for centuries. We serve it with a sprinkle of brown sugar and raisins and a pat of butter."

Owen likes oatmeal. So does his granddad. That is what they order. Owen sees *skyr* on the menu and he orders that, too.

While eating, Owen's granddad consults Gunnar's map of Iceland, which he has pulled from his briefcase, and traces the route with his finger.

"According to this map, Stephansson grew up on a farm on the northern coast here, where a monument has been placed. Gunnar would want us to visit it. Fortunately, the monument is close to where our archive is located."

"Sounds good, Pops," Owen says, his heart skipping a beat at the mention of the archive.

Owen's granddad pays for breakfast with his credit card. Then they wheel their luggage to the car-rental agency, which is three blocks away. It's still early in the morning so they are the first customers. They get served right away.

"*Velkominn.* Can I help you?" the rental clerk asks in an accent that Owen is getting used to.

Owen's granddad explains that they will need a car for the weekend just as another customer arrives, a tall, blonde woman wearing a ponytail and large, round sunglasses. She stands to the side politely listening to their story while consulting her cell phone from time to time.

The rental clerk begins the paperwork.

"May I have your driver's license, please?" she asks.

Owen's granddad reaches into his briefcase and roots through it. His movements get more and more frantic. Then he pats down his coat pockets. He comes up empty.

"Did you forget it?" Owen asks.

His granddad barely nods. He seems dumbstruck.

Owen turns to the rental clerk.

"I can vouch for my granddad. He has a driver's license. That's how we got to the airport back in Canada."

"I'm so sorry. We can't rent a car without proof of a driver's license. It's the law."

"Are you sure you don't have it, Pops?" Owen asks. "Maybe you tucked it away somewhere safe like you told me to do with the money."

"Help me look," he says.

They step aside to let the ponytail woman go ahead while Owen helps empty out everything in his granddad's briefcase and coat pockets.

They stop rummaging at the same time.

They stare at each other. Owen blinks like an owl.

No driver's license.

SEVEN

Owen's granddad collapses in a chair near the car rental's front counter. He is gray and stricken. Speechless. The forgotten driver's license leaves him staring at the polished floor while Owen stands helplessly beside him, a fist-sized lump in his throat.

The disappointment hits Owen, too. He is not going to be able to retrieve his notebook after all.

The emptied briefcase tumbles to the floor. Owen picks it up and places it on the chair beside his granddad, who doesn't seem to notice.

"At least you were able to return Gunnar's medal," Owen consoles him while placing a hand on his granddad's sagging shoulder.

His granddad says nothing. He hangs his head even lower.

Only then does Owen realize his mistake.

For Owen's granddad, this trip isn't about returning the Order of the Falcon. This trip is about proving something to Owen's mom and dad, to the ladies from the Red Deer River Readers Book Club, and maybe especially to Owen.

And now Owen's granddad has failed.

Failed terribly.

Owen doesn't know what to do. He doesn't know what to say. He is numb. What is their next move? He has no idea.

The clerk behind the counter hands car keys to the ponytail woman. She turns to study Owen and his granddad while holding the keys in her hand.

"I'm sorry to hear about your troubles," the ponytail woman says with an Icelandic accent, removing her sunglasses. "Where were you two headed?"

Owen's granddad recovers slightly and clears his throat.

"The northern coast," he says, "but only over-night. We have to be back in Canada on Sunday."

"I think you're in luck. *I'm* headed to the northern coast. Perhaps you'd like to join me for the first part of my trip, and I can see if someone in my office at Akureyri will be headed to Reykjavík and can drive you back in time for your flight home."

"Are you sure?" Neville says, brightening up considerably.

"Absolutely. I could use the company. My name is Aris Magnúsdóttir," she says, holding out her hand to shake. "I work for the cultural ministry here in Iceland."

They introduce themselves. She turns to Owen.

"I believe I saw you at the airport this morning," Aris says. "You were chatting with my little girl, Britta."

The girl with baby teeth and crooked pigtails, Owen thinks.

"What a happy coincidence," Neville says.

Aris shrugs.

"We're a very small country. Everyone knows everyone in Iceland. Are those your bags?" she asks, pointing to their luggage.

They nod eagerly.

"Well, then. Let's be on our way."

It is not long before they are on the highway, making their way up the coast, the endless gray ocean always appearing on their left-hand side. They learn that Aris is meeting with various councils who want to improve their villages so that they can attract more tourists to their area. And Aris knows plenty about Iceland, which she is happy to share.

Aris tells them that Iceland is made up of only 320,000 people and that 200,000 of them live in the capital city of Reykjavík. She tells them that Reykjavík is the northernmost capital in the world. She says that Reykjavík means smoky bay and is so named because of the steam or "smoke" that was rising from the land when the first settlers arrived over a thousand years ago.

Owen tries to follow along, but he floats in and out of her stories. He's relieved that they are able to continue their journey, but he keeps thinking about the missing driver's license that nearly jeopardized their plans. He wonders if his granddad has forgotten anything else that they will need on this trip.

A small animal darts across the road.

"That's an Arctic fox," Aris says, looking at Owen through her rearview mirror. "It is the only native animal of Iceland."

Owen snaps out of his worries and presses his face against the window, but the fox has disappeared among the orange lichen-covered lava fields.

They enter a dark tunnel.

"We'll be going under the sea now," Aris says. "This tunnel is six kilometers long, but it is a short-cut between two points of land."

"How cold is the water?" Owen asks.

"Very," Aris says. "Even in the summer the ocean is barely five degrees Celsius."

"Brrrrrrr!" Neville says. "That would certainly fail the big-toe test!"

"The big-toe test?" Aris asks, puzzled.

"He means when you test the water with your bare foot before going in," Owen explains from the backseat.

Aris laughs. Owen's pleased to see that he and his granddad can entertain her.

When they come out of the tunnel, they are surrounded by desolate rocky moors studded with deep blue pools. Owen digs out his camera to try to capture the landscape's dark mood. Aris spies him with his camera in the rearview mirror.

"Iceland certainly inspires writers and photographers," she says.

"That's why we're here," Neville says. "My late friend Gunnar received the Order of the Falcon for his work translating one of your poets. We returned his medal in Reykjavík and now we're delivering his notes to an archive on the northern coast."

"Which poet?" Aris asks.

"Stephan G. Stephansson," Neville says.

"Ah! He's one of our country's best," Aris says. "There's a monument dedicated to him near the town of Sauðárkrókur."

"That's right," Neville says. "It's where our archive is located, according to my friend's map."

"I know one of the archivists who works there," Aris says. "You see? Everyone knows everyone in Iceland."

Aris slows the car down.

"Do you mind if we take a short detour to stop at my favorite natural wonder?" she asks.

"Not at all!" Neville says. He turns around to face Owen. "Isn't this grand?"

Owen only nods, because now he's thinking about his notebook at the archive once again.

Aris pulls off the main road onto a country lane. They drive a bit farther. Free-roaming sheep bleat on both sides of the road. Aris has to slow down whenever one of them threatens to dart across. After a few more minutes, she pulls into a small gravel parking lot.

They pile out of the car and are hit by a rotten egg smell as if someone has struck a match. Clouds of billowing steam rise ahead.

"Phew!" Owen says, waving at his nose.

Aris laughs as she leads them to the row of angry steaming vents. When they draw closer, they see boiling water spewing up from the ground, making loud belching sounds. There are posted signs warning to stand back from harm's way. The warm, billowing steam envelops them. They can barely see each other. Owen pulls out his camera but discovers that it is impossible to take photographs without fogging up his lens.

"This is the biggest hot spring in Europe. Water comes from deep inside the earth," Aris says above the roaring vents. "It's what we use to heat our homes and our geothermal pools."

Owen thinks back to what the flight attendant on the airplane told him, but then he frowns because he remembers the confused scene on the flight with his granddad.

Owen stands in the fog and slowly turns a full circle so that everything is a blur. The foul air fills his lungs, and the roar of the belching steam vents carries away the voices around him. He becomes disoriented, which scares him a little. Is this how his granddad sometimes feels?

Owen steps out of the thick steam to clear his head and turns to face thunderclouds that are forming in the distance. He spots something through his lens.

"Lightning," Owen says as he lowers his camera to better view the deepening skies.

Aris and Owen's granddad step away from the steaming vents to look. Another bolt strikes, followed by the low rumble of thunder that they can feel in their feet. They hurry to the car and continue down the road back to the main highway as the first raindrops hit the windshield.

"This will blow over quickly," Aris assures them.

"Like a Canadian prairie storm," Neville says.

"But not so deadly," Aris adds.

"Deadly? What do you mean?" Owen asks from the backseat.

"Have you read about Stephansson's son, Gestur?" Aris asks.

She studies Owen in the rearview mirror briefly before returning her attention to the road.

Owen gulps. Of course he knows about Stephansson's son. It was well covered during his field trip. The terrible event. The subsequent poem. Everything.

"I didn't know he had a son," Neville says when Owen doesn't reply.

Owen fidgets in the backseat but no one notices.

"Five sons and three daughters altogether," Aris says. "He wrote a particularly heartfelt poem about the one named Gestur at his farm in Alberta. I think of that poem every time I see lightning."

"How does it go?" Neville asks.

Before Owen can stop her, Aris begins to recite.

"The law which cuts life's thinly ravelled thread,
Gave little time for dread or hope or sadness.
It flung a bolt from heaven overhead
And felled my cherished son in its blind
     madness."

Aris drives on. Electric silence fills the car. Owen holds his breath.

"So Gestur was struck by lightning," Neville says, piecing the poem's clues together.

"Tragically, yes," Aris confirms. "It happened in the summer during the early 1900s. Two of Stephansson's sons, Gestur and Jakob, were running home ahead of the storm with their friend Bjorn. Gestur was the last of the three to reach the wire fence just as lightning struck. He died instantly. He was only sixteen. That night, his grief-stricken father wrote those words."

"So sad," Neville says. "How does the rest of the poem go?"

"No!" Owen erupts from the backseat. "No! I ... I don't want to hear any more!"

Startled, his granddad turns around to face Owen.

"Are you okay?" he asks.

"I just ... let's talk about something else," Owen manages to sputter, frantic thoughts colliding.

His granddad stares at him for a long minute before returning to face the front.

Owen's heart is roaring in his ears while his granddad quietly explains something to Aris about Owen's grandmother dying a year ago.

"I'm so sorry for your loss," Aris says to Neville. She looks at Owen in her rearview mirror. "I didn't know, Owen. My apologies."

Owen nods, then stares out the window to steady himself.

The rain is coming down hard, dancing across the highway in sheets and forcing Aris to slow down. The car's wipers slap away at the windshield. Then, just as suddenly as the rain starts, it begins to peter out and the skies brighten.

"You see? The weather always lets up," Aris says, sounding overly cheerful to compensate for Owen's unexpected outburst.

Owen gives her a fleeting smile to let her know that he's feeling better, which he is now that Stephansson's poem is off-limits.

Outside Owen's window, rolling hills peppered with sheep and moss-dressed rocks sail by. The car's heater is on because it is only eight degrees Celsius outside. There are no trees for as far as Owen can see, and only occasionally do farmhouses appear, all of the white-with-red-roof variety.

"It looks so lonely out here," Owen observes, taking photographs of the land that echo the emptiness.

"I think there's a fine line between a barren lonely place and somewhere that's starkly beautiful," Aris says.

Owen thinks about this while studying the photographs he just took. Encouraged, he takes some more, trying to capture the beauty that Aris sees. But finally the travel catches up to Owen. He falls asleep in the backseat and everything goes black.

EIGHT

After Owen and his granddad have been driving with Aris for another hour, they pass a road sign that reads *Blönduós*. Aris slows down for some crossing sheep, and Owen wakes up.

"Blönduós is the first major town we'll come to on the northern coast. We'll stop there for the night. Then we'll only have another fifty kilometers to go before we get to Sauðárkrókur, where your archive is located and the region where Stephansson's family first farmed," Aris says.

"As I recall, Stephansson moved to Alberta in 1888, along with eleven other Icelandic families. My friend Gunnar traced his roots back to one of those families," Neville says.

He turns in his seat to face Owen.

"Owen, think about Alberta back then. No highways or bridges. No electricity. No grocery stores."

Owen's stomach growls.

"And no restaurants," Owen adds.

"Speaking of restaurants, who's hungry?" Aris asks, taking the hint.

"Me!" Owen says. It has been a long time since they ate breakfast in Reykjavík.

"I know a great little place up ahead." Aris says. "It's called the Peckish Arctic Tern, named after a popular seabird in Iceland."

They pass a scenic lookout with crashing waves that pummel craggy black rocks below and pull into a small parking lot in front of a wooden-clad café.

"I hope you like seafood chowder. That's the specialty here," Aris says as she climbs out of the car. "They make it with char."

"What's char?" Owen whispers to his granddad.

"Fish," Neville explains, holding the café door open for Owen and Aris.

Owen slows his steps, but his granddad ushers him inside.

The walls are decorated with rusty fishing gear, and a glass milk bottle filled with water and lemons has been placed on each table. The tables are made of old painted doors laid flat on wooden legs, and the chairs are mismatched but comfortable-looking. They sit down next to the large front window.

Owen is relieved to see that hamburgers are also on the menu, but both Owen's granddad and Aris order the specialty.

While they wait for their food, Aris steps outside to make some work-related calls. Owen and his granddad watch her through the window as she paces back and forth while talking and sometimes laughing with whomever she is speaking to.

"Aris is really nice," Owen remarks.

"Indeed," Neville says. "I see you've been taking lots of photos."

Owen pulls out his camera from his knapsack and clicks through the images he has taken that day: the boiling steam vents, the distant snow-capped mountains and the sheep. Always the sheep. He shares the screen with his granddad who nods his approval.

When Aris returns, she says she has some wonderful news.

"I've arranged for the archivist I know to show you some of Stephansson's documents in their collection. You'll be able to see his handwritten letters from Alberta firsthand!"

"When?" Owen blurts at the mention of the archive.

"Tomorrow morning. But before that, I thought I'd take you to a nearby geothermal pool since no trip to Iceland is complete without one. Then we'll have time to visit a historic turf-walled farmhouse and church. That will give you a good sense of the conditions that Stephansson's family lived in before leaving Iceland for North America."

"Terrific!" Neville says. "These are all the things that Gunnar would have loved for us to see."

Aris nods, but she's not done.

"From there, I'll drop you off at the archive while I attend to some meetings. After that, I'll deliver you to Stephansson's monument and I'll be on my way. My colleagues Ragna Guðmundsdóttir and Oddny Thorvaldson from Akureyri will drive you back in time for your flight home."

"Do they have meetings in Reykjavík?" Neville asks.

"They do."

"What a perfect plan! We can't thank you enough," Neville exclaims.

Owen also beams. His notebook is within reach. He allows himself to believe that nothing can go wrong now.

Their server arrives with the meals and he lays down soup spoons beside the two bowls of chowder. While he does so, Owen takes a huge bite of his hamburger. It is delicious, just like at home.

Owen reaches for the ketchup and squeezes some onto his plate beside his fries. As he puts the ketchup bottle back on the table, he notices that his granddad has picked up his spoon and is staring at it.

"What's wrong with the spoon?" Owen asks.

"The spoon?" Neville repeats. "Is that what this is?"

Owen looks at the spoon in his granddad's hand. The spoon is as ordinary as they come.

"Of course it's a spoon," Owen says.

"What's it for?" Neville asks.

His granddad must be joking, Owen thinks.

Only, his granddad isn't. He is waiting for an answer.

"It's for your chowder," Owen says, frowning.

His granddad sets the spoon down. He picks up his fork.

"What are you doing?" Owen asks.

"What do you mean?" Neville asks.

"You're going to use your fork to eat chowder?"

Owen's granddad looks down at his meal. He has that confused look again. Then he stares at Owen as if he has no idea where he is.

"The spoon would work better," Owen says, blinking like an owl.

Owen takes another bite of his hamburger. He does not want to make a big deal out of something as ridiculous as cutlery. He steals a glance at Aris. He sees that she has been quietly watching the scene, but she takes Owen's lead and starts eating her chowder as if nothing peculiar has happened.

"Can you taste the char?" she asks Owen's granddad between spoonfuls.

Owen's granddad cautiously picks up his spoon and tries a mouthful.

"Yes. It's excellent," he declares.

They eat their meals in awkward silence.

"How is everything?" the server asks after he swoops back to check on them.

"Good."

"Terrific."

"Delicious."

All three speak at once, breaking the tension.

Aris talks about her work and the meetings that she has lined up over the next few days. She is planning to circle all the way around Iceland on a highway called the Ring Road before heading back to Reykjavík.

"Back to Reykjavík and my little Britta," she says longingly.

They order dessert. Owen's granddad and Aris

each order a slice of bilberry pie, which his grand-dad reports tastes like blueberries. Owen orders his favorite, rhubarb crisp. It is not as good as his grandmother's, but he finishes it anyway, scraping his plate clean. Owen's granddad scoops up the bill when the server lays it on their table.

"This meal is on me, Aris," Neville declares. "We're so grateful for all you've done."

"It's nothing," Aris says with a dismissive wave of her hand. "I'm glad to have the company." Then she adds tentatively, "They only take cash here. Do you have Icelandic currency?"

Owen's granddad starts to search his pockets, but Owen stops him.

"Pops. You gave me the envelope of money. Remember?"

Owen pulls out the envelope stuffed with Ice-landic bills from his knapsack as proof. He starts to hand it to his granddad, but his granddad gently pushes the envelope back to Owen.

"Let's see if you can figure out how much to pay," Neville suggests.

Before Owen can answer, his granddad turns to Aris and starts talking about her two colleagues who will be meeting them tomorrow at Stephans-son's monument. Owen gets up and moves to the cash register near the door.

Owen isn't too worried about figuring out how much to pay. As he pulls out the money from the envelope, he can see that Icelandic currency comes in bills of five hundred, one thousand, two thousand and five thousand, so it's easy to count like Canadian money.

Still. He wonders how his grandad would fare with the math. Would his granddad have trouble? Is that why Owen got the job?

Things are adding up in a way that Owen doesn't like. His granddad is forgetting important things like a driver's license. He is confusing routine things like cutlery. He is getting lost, like when they were on the airplane.

What's happening?

Owen looks over at his granddad who is talking to Aris and making her laugh.

Nothing is wrong, Owen tries to assure himself. Nothing.

So how come there's a knot in his stomach?

When they leave the café and climb back into the car, Aris tells them that she has also arranged for accommodations.

"I've booked us rooms at my favorite inn in this area," she says. "It's called the Ambitious Viking Guest House."

"What an unusual name," Neville says.

"Not so much," Aris says. "Almost everyone who's Icelandic can trace their roots back to the Vikings."

When they pull up to the guest house, it is still light out, but their shadows stretch long before them. Owen remembers what his granddad told him about the sun not setting at this time of year. Now he wonders if he will be able to sleep with it being so bright outside.

They enter through the front doors and meet the innkeeper.

"How do you like Iceland?" she asks when she learns that Owen and his granddad are from Canada.

"It's been quite an adventure," Neville says, "for two old-timers like us."

The innkeeper chuckles. She turns to Owen.

"And what have you enjoyed the most?"

Owen does not hesitate.

"Photographing the landscapes," he declares. "The sky. The weather. The light. I think I must have taken dozens of pictures by now."

"I've never been to Canada," the innkeeper says. "What does the landscape look like where you live?"

"Flat," Owen says. "We're from the prairies." But he thinks some more, and in his mind's eye he can see a cathedral-high blue sky. He can see the rolling thunderstorms that can change the weather in minutes, the light when the harvest moon colors the fields with shards of silver and the blinding white sparkles that drift down to form the banks of softly fallen snow.

"But our skies are beautiful," Owen adds.

Owen's granddad smiles at him with pride.

"We have you staying with us for one night," the innkeeper says, checking her records. "What are you planning to visit in our district?"

"The archive," Owen blurts. It's still his number-one priority.

"At Sauðárkrókur," Aris adds.

"We're going there to donate notes from my late friend Gunnar Ingvarsson who translated much of Stephan G. Stephansson's poetry," Neville explains.

"Ah! Stephansson! So you'll be sure to visit his monument," the innkeeper says.

"Indeed! That's our final destination," Neville says.

Owen glances at his granddad. The determined tone in his voice catches Owen off guard.

"We'll go there tomorrow morning after a dip at Reykir. We'll also be visiting the turf houses in Glaumbær, as well as the turf church at Varmahlíð," Aris adds.

"Well done," the innkeeper says, clapping her hands. "You'll cover all of Stephansson's sites."

"I like the name of your inn," Owen says. "Do you come from Vikings?" he asks. "Like Aris?"

The innkeeper laughs.

"Not me, I'm afraid," she says. "But I married an Icelander who can trace his roots that far back. We opened this inn together right after we were married."

The innkeeper turns the register to face her guests.

"Please sign in here," she says, pointing to an empty line on the register. "I'll need your name, your nationality, your address and a phone number."

"You sign for us," Neville says to Owen, nudging him.

Owen uses his best handwriting and completes all the fields. His granddad checks his work and nods with approval.

"Breakfast is served between 7:00 and 10:00 a.m.," the innkeeper tells them when she hands out the room keys.

"Sleep well. I'll see you in the morning," Aris says to them both, and she heads to her room on the second floor.

Owen and his granddad climb to the third floor with their luggage. When they get to their room, number six, Owen is thrilled to see that they have the top-floor room with a balcony. He throws his knapsack onto one of the twin beds and steps outside. His granddad joins him at the railing.

It is quiet. Most of the buildings around them are a soft pinkish-white. In the distance, they can see the snow-capped mountains with flattened tops and a swift glacial river cutting through the town in search of the cold, vast sea.

A wave of tiredness hits Owen even though it is still light out. He yawns.

"I'm bushed, as well," Neville says. "Let's get some shut-eye."

Owen is too played out to brush his teeth, but his granddad makes him anyway. When he washes his face, the hot water from the tap smells like the angry vents he breathed in earlier that day. He asks about it, and his granddad reminds him that the smell is due to the geothermal springs, hot water from deep underground, but that it is perfectly safe to drink.

Owen puts on his rodeo pajamas and crawls into bed with its crisp white sheets and puffy feather duvet. The next thing he knows, he wakes up to the sound of the door to their room quietly shutting.

He bolts up in bed.

"Pops?" he calls out, turning to his granddad's bed.

But his granddad is gone.

NINE

Owen shuts the door to their guest room, having learned that the outside hallway is empty and his granddad is nowhere in sight. He glances around for clues as to where his granddad might be headed in the middle of the night. Even with the curtains pulled across the balcony doors, it is still bright enough inside to see.

Owen spots his granddad's coat, which had been tossed on a nearby chair, so he knows his granddad has not gone far. Not outside anyway. Perhaps he wanted to ask the innkeeper a question about their room? Perhaps he was hungry and went downstairs to pick out something from the fruit bowl beside the register at the front desk? Perhaps he forgot something in the car — Gunnar's map, maybe?

These are all perfectly logical explanations. Still, with everything that has been going on with his granddad, Owen decides to wait up for his return. To distract himself, he digs out his camera and lies down on his bed to look at his photographs of Iceland. Then he returns to the file of photographs of Stephansson House. He clicks through and pauses on a photograph he took of one of Stephansson's portraits.

In it, Stephansson is wearing a double-breasted jacket, perhaps the best jacket he owns. He is younger, maybe Owen's dad's age, and he is staring off to the right and a little downward. His gaze is soft, slightly unfocused. He looks as if he is not even aware of the camera. What is he thinking about? It has to be something bigger than feeding his livestock. Bigger than planting crops to harvest. Bigger than stocking his root cellar for the winter.

And then Owen knows. Stephansson is thinking about his next poem. His next poem is what keeps Stephansson going, almost like the food on his table. His poems are what keep him connected to everything and everyone around him. His poems are what give him a bigger purpose and make him happy to be alive, happy enough even to nail a crescent moon to the trim of his house. His poems are what will be recited by generations to follow, giving Stephansson a voice long after he is gone.

Owen sets his camera aside. Stephansson feels more real to him now. He wonders what Stephansson would think about the things Owen wrote in his notebook. Stephansson might be as disappointed as Owen's granddad would be, Owen thinks.

Owen sighs. He pulls back his duvet and walks to the balcony doors to view the glacial river that is rushing by. The floor creaks beneath his bare feet. He opens the curtains. All is quiet. Nothing moves except the river. Then voices.

Owen turns to the door of their room. His granddad walks in along with Aris. Neville is dressed, but Aris is in her housecoat and slippers.

"What's going on?" Owen asks.

He has a sinking feeling. His granddad has that confused look again. Neville crosses the room and slowly sits down on the edge of his bed but says nothing.

Owen looks to Aris.

"I was watching TV in the guest lounge downstairs," Aris explains, her voice unnaturally cheerful for this late hour. "I miss Britta. I couldn't sleep. And in walks your granddad. I think I might have had the volume up too loudly."

"Yes, I heard the TV," Neville confirms. "I wanted to see if the news was on. I always watch the news before I go to bed."

Owen knows that this is true. Whenever he stayed over at his grandparents' home, his bedtime was scheduled with the start of the late-night news. He would kiss them good night as they sat together in the living room — his granddad on the sofa, his grandmother in her orange recliner — then climb to his bedroom attic where he'd listen through the floorboards to the day's events until he was lulled to sleep.

"So we watched TV for a bit," Aris says. "There was a story about new airline rules for luggage. And then ..." Aris hesitates.

"I couldn't remember where I put my suitcase," Neville cuts in. His voice is clearer now, his eyes more focused.

"What do you mean?" Owen asks. "It's right there."

Owen points to his granddad's suitcase that is standing near the door to their bathroom, unopened since their arrival at the guest house.

"That's not mine," Neville declares.

"Yes it is," Owen says. "Mine's over here."

He points to his own suitcase, which is lying

122

open beside his bed, the contents spilling out onto the floor.

His granddad looks dubious.

"Well okay, then. Let's open *that* suitcase. We'll make sure it's *your* stuff inside," Owen suggests.

This is the notebook mix-up all over again, Owen thinks. He has to open the cover to prove his point.

His granddad reluctantly nods.

Owen retrieves the other suitcase and heaves it onto his granddad's bed. He unzips it and throws back the cover.

Owen blinks, owl-like.

Aris takes a step closer to peer inside. She puts her hand to her mouth.

Owen stares with alarm into his granddad's face.

His granddad looks away.

"Oops," Neville says quietly. "It appears as if I didn't do a very good job packing."

"No," Owen says in a little voice. "You didn't."

Inside the suitcase are his granddad's socks.

Just socks.

All socks.

A suitcase full of socks.

"Well, I must be off to bed," Aris says quietly.

But before she leaves, she gives Owen a gentle squeeze on his arm.

"We'll chat in the morning," she says kindly.

She softly closes the door behind her. The silence she leaves in her wake is deafening. They can hear the tick of the alarm clock on the night table, the distant thrumming of the glacial river rushing by and birds still singing because the sun refuses to go down.

"Pops?" Owen says.

"My feet get cold," Neville replies.

"What about pajamas?" Owen asks.

"I guess I forgot them. I had a lot on my mind. All those last-minute travel details," Neville says.

"Right," Owen says. "You had a lot to remember."

He wants so badly to believe his granddad. He tries to convince himself that having to quickly plan for a short trip to another country might explain a suitcase full of socks.

But it's no use.

"We'd better get some sleep," Neville says. "We have another full day tomorrow before we head home."

"Right," Owen says again, turning away.

Owen knows he is still doing his blinking thing. He can't help it. He is also having trouble with his words. He crawls into his bed and pulls the duvet over himself. He closes his eyes and listens to the sounds of his granddad who is also getting ready for bed. After a few minutes of silence, he opens one eye to spy on his granddad.

His granddad is lying on his own bed, glasses and shoes removed but otherwise fully clothed with his duvet half-thrown over his body. He is staring up at the ceiling, one arm tucked under his head. He looks uncomfortable.

Owen gulps down his sadness. He rolls over to face the other way, snuggling into his pajamas, the ones he so carefully chose to bring. For the first time since the beginning of their adventure, Owen misses home.

When Owen wakes up, he is not sure what time it is because the light has not changed all that much inside their room. But it is morning. His granddad is in the bathroom. Owen can hear the shower going and his granddad whistling some happy tune, as if last night with the suitcase full of socks never happened.

Owen stretches and climbs out of bed. He throws back the curtains of the balcony doors and squints up at the bright gray sky. Then he changes into clean clothes, trying hard not to think about his granddad's suitcase.

Owen's granddad emerges from the bathroom wielding a toothbrush. Although he has showered, he has had to change back into his clothing from the day before.

"Bathroom's all yours," Neville announces as if everything is right with the world.

"Where did you get the toothbrush?" Owen asks.

"The innkeeper gave me some spare supplies," he says proudly. "Problem solved."

"That's great," Owen says.

But Owen is wary. Owen is on guard.

He uses the bathroom. When he is done, his granddad is waiting to take him downstairs where they will have breakfast with Aris. She joins them shortly after they sit down in the dining room. Its walls are covered with photographs of sparkling pale blue glaciers breaking off into the dull gray Arctic Ocean.

"Did you sleep well?" Aris asks them brightly.

"Yes," they both say together, Owen a beat behind his granddad.

The server arrives with coffee and then their meals.

Owen worries when he sees spoons on the table, but his granddad picks one up to stir sugar into his coffee as if he has been using spoons all his life.

Which he has, Owen thinks.

His granddad takes a healthy slurp of his coffee and then smiles at both of them.

Aris does not mention the suitcase full of socks, but Owen catches her staring at Owen from time to time. He focuses on getting his food down, hoping it will take away the cramps in his stomach.

It doesn't.

After breakfast, they check out of the inn and climb into Aris's car. All luggage is accounted for. Owen secretly makes sure of that. It is a short drive to Reykir where they will go for an outdoor swim. To their right is the ocean, today steel blue, and in the distance a solitary island looms with steep cliffs all around.

"That's Drangey," Aris announces.

Owen, who has been stewing in the backseat, now looks out his window. He has seen this striking island before. Then he remembers where.

"Stephansson has a painting of that island at his homestead in Alberta," Owen reports.

His granddad turns to give him a pleased nod.

"Take a photo," Neville suggests.

Owen tries to take a shot that makes the island look strong and defiant like the painting that Stephansson owned, but his hands shake and the photograph comes out blurry. He deletes it.

"Here we are," Aris says as she pulls into a parking lot, which is practically empty because of the early hour and the remoteness of the place.

She retrieves a small tote bag from her trunk.

"All Icelanders travel with their swimsuits, but if you didn't pack yours, you can rent one."

The mention of packing reminds Owen of the suitcase full of socks. Now he can't stop thinking about it.

They enter a small wooden building that sells hot coffee and knot-shaped pastries along with tickets to the outdoor pools. Owen and his granddad are directed to the men's changing area, which is back outside in a fenced enclosure. Gusty cold wind blows right off the Arctic waters, making it a challenge to get undressed. Once changed, they make a dash for the two pools. Each is shaped like a large well and surrounded by flat stones. Owen spots a set of stairs that leads into the closest pool where Aris is already immersed.

"Hot! Hot! Hot!" he yelps as he descends the steps in his haste to get out of the cold wind.

Aris laughs.

"You're right. It's forty degrees Celsius. You'll soon get used to it."

Owen and his granddad slowly ease into the water and eventually settle down on the rocky ledge that serves as a bench all around the pool. Arctic gusts blast their bright pink faces, but they are warm beneath the surface.

"I've never felt better," Neville declares.

Owen says nothing.

They stay in the pool for half an hour, staring out at the lone island of Drangey or behind them at the black mountain face called Tindastóll, letting the heat soak deep into their bones.

Owen tries to relax. He can't.

After Reykir, they take a short drive to the historic farm at Glaumbær where they scramble out of the car. The farm is made up of a row of little turf houses with white wood fronts and sod roofs that go from the peak all the way to the ground. The windows are tiny and few.

They go inside. The lighting is almost cave-like. The buildings are connected by narrow tunnels. The ceilings are low. The floor is packed dirt. The air smells like earth, like they are buried.

"People used to live here?" Neville asks in wonder.

"Right up until 1947," Aris says. "Stephansson's parents were married at this very site," she adds.

They stand in what looks to Owen like the bedroom. There are two rows of small wood-framed beds with woven wool covers along the walls. A clothes trunk and a spinning wheel stand at the far end of the room.

Owen barely takes in the homespun details, but his granddad points to Owen's camera, so he shoots some photographs in his numbed state. The photographs look exactly the way he feels.

Flat.

He deletes them, too.

Next, they visit the nearby turf church, a national historic site near Stephansson's family farm at Varmahlíð.

It is also tiny. The walkway is stone. The front is clad with dark wood and two red-trimmed windows on either side of a turquoise-painted door. At the peak is a plain wood cross. The walls are made of sod like the farmhouses, with tufts of grass sticking out everywhere. Inside are rows of straight wooden benches with a central aisle and a pulpit at the front.

"This church owned the land that Stephansson's family farmed in this region," Aris explains. "Every spring, his family would have to make a payment of eight sheep to the church to cover rent, and every summer they had to pay five kilos of butter. It was a small fortune back then."

Owen is having trouble concentrating. Maybe fresh air would help. He bolts outside. He finds himself standing in a little graveyard behind the church. The tombstones remind him of old people sitting in crooked lawn chairs at a country barbecue, all facing the same way to watch a game of horseshoes but gossiping among themselves.

It is getting close to eleven in the morning, so they head to their last stop before Stephansson's monument: the Skagafjörður Archive.

Owen perks up.

His notebook!

With all his worries about his granddad, Owen almost forgot why he wanted to go to Iceland in the first place.

The archivist is waiting for them at the front doors and gives Aris a giant hug when they arrive.

"So great to see you," the archivist says jovially. "How's little Britta?"

"Just fine," Aris says. "My mom's staying with her."

Aris introduces Owen and his granddad to the archivist.

"And you were friends with one of Stephansson's very best literary translators, Gunnar Ingvarsson," she said, turning to Owen's granddad. "Thank you so much for sending Stephansson's travel journal. We've received it safe and sound."

"I'm certain Gunnar would be pleased that you have it. I've also brought his notes about the journal,"

Neville says, patting his briefcase. "I thought you might like that, too."

"Wonderful! Well, come with me. I know you don't have much time, so I've already pulled out the documents that we have by Stephansson. You'll be able to see why his travel journal is such an important addition to our collection."

"I'll be back in an hour," Aris reminds Owen and his granddad.

She returns to her car to head to her meeting.

Owen and his granddad follow the archivist into a special reading room on the second floor, and she leads them to a large white table. On it are three bundles of documents wrapped with cardboard covers and brown paper, tied shut with cotton straps. The archivist unties the first bundle and opens the folder inside.

"We don't have a lot of documents by Stephansson because most of them are housed at the national archive in Reykjavík," she says.

The archivist produces the marbled blue travel journal that Owen's granddad couriered.

"It's a beautiful artifact," she says, almost transfixed by what she is holding.

Then the archivist unwraps the next bundle and shows them pages of handwritten letters that are a hundred years old. It is hard for Owen to read cursive writing and it is especially hard because the words are in Icelandic. But every so often, Owen spots English place-names that nearly jump off the pages: Canada, Alberta, Edmonton, Calgary, Red Deer, Markerville, Swan Lake and Medicine River.

Seeing these familiar names makes Owen ache. On top of everything else, his homesickness is worsening.

The archivist opens up the last bundle. This one contains letters by Stephansson, all in Icelandic, only the writing is very different, very child-like. The words are larger, jagged and crooked on the page. They are written in what looks like a thick purple pencil, not the elegant black fountain pen and razor-sharp lines of the earlier letters. A lot of the sentences are aggressively crossed out with Stephansson starting again and again in shaky penmanship, as if he is chasing his words. It looks like he wrote these letters with his left hand.

"What's going on?" Owen asks.

"Stephansson had a stroke in the months just before he died," the archivist explains. "Think of how frustrating it must have been for him to be at the height of his creativity and filled with so much poetry, but to have such a difficult time writing it down. In some ways, these letters touch me the most."

Owen's granddad picks up one of the purple-penciled letters.

"I can see why. He's desperate to be heard," Neville says quietly.

"How can you tell?" Owen asks.

Owen's granddad points to the paragraph right before Stephansson's signature.

Each of the last three scrambled sentences ends in a bold exclamation mark.

!

!

!

Neville points to each exclamation mark and declares, "I am here. I am here. I am still here."

Owen takes a step back as if he has been slapped in the face with each punctuation mark. He can practically feel Stephansson pointing an accusing finger at him right there in the room.

Owen's knees almost buckle with the overwhelming guilt that he has been carrying. He stands numb as the archivist begins to put Stephansson's work back into the protective folders with great care.

Owen's granddad pulls out Gunnar's notebook from his briefcase.

"Here is Gunnar's research about Stephansson's travel journal," he says, handing the yellow notebook to the archivist with equal care. "And in exchange," he adds, shooting Owen a smile, "do you happen to have my grandson's notebook? It looks like this one, only it's green."

TEN

Owen comes out of his haze at the mention of his notebook.

"Ah, yes. Your grandson's notebook," the archivist says to Neville, taking Gunnar's notebook from his hands.

She turns to Owen. "You did a beautiful job recording field notes about Stephansson House. I dream about going to Alberta one day and visiting that historic site myself, so I read what you wrote from cover to cover. I'll go get it. It's in my office."

When she leaves the room, Owen turns to face his granddad.

"Pops," he says.

"Yes?"

Now is the time to confess. Only Owen has no words.

"Something wrong?" Neville asks, bending a little to look into Owen's face.

Owen opens his mouth but nothing comes out. He can only blink, his left eye slower than the right.

"Owen?" Neville asks, his eyebrows raised in concern.

"Here you are," the archivist says brightly as soon as she re-enters the room.

Even from where Owen stands, he can see that she has the right notebook. It is green.

The archivist strides toward them, holding his notebook out.

"I also enjoyed the poetry exercises that followed your field notes. Similes. Metaphors. Hyperbole. Personification. Alliteration. Onomatopoeia. But I must ask you, Owen. Did you write the poem on the last page?"

Owen tries to swallow. His ears are burning up. The backs of his knees are sweating.

"A poem?" Neville says, turning to Owen. "Is it the one about your grandmother? The one you read at her funeral?"

Owen gives a weak nod. He stares at his shoes.

"It's a wonderful poem," Neville says to the archivist. "Everyone said so at the funeral. The things Owen wrote! You can imagine how proud we were."

Neville reaches to take the notebook from the archivist, but Owen is quicker. He snatches it from her and without a word, flees from the room, down the stairs and out the front doors. He only stops when he spots a bench off to the side near the empty parking lot. He collapses on it, drops his notebook to the ground and puts his head in his hands.

Moments later, he feels his granddad sit down beside him.

"I thanked the archivist for both of us," Neville mentions quietly. "She wants to you have this."

Owen manages to look up to see his granddad holding out a pen. Owen takes it. It has *Skagafjörður Archive* printed on its side. A souvenir.

Owen says nothing as he puts it into his pocket. He wipes his eyes and puts his head back in his hands, staring at the grass between his feet. The pages of his discarded notebook blow open and turn in the soft breeze.

"I'm so sorry about your grandmother. I know how you feel. I miss her, too," Neville says. "We all do."

"No," Owen manages to say.

"No?" Neville asks.

"I miss her. I miss Grandma every day. But it's not that."

"What is it, then?"

Owen takes a deep breath. He sits up to face his granddad.

"The poem I read at her funeral? That wasn't my poem. Not completely."

"Oh?"

"I tried. I really tried. I wanted it to be perfect for her. But I couldn't finish it. I couldn't finish the ending. And so I copied a few verses from another poem. Stephansson's poem. The one about his son who died from the lightning bolt."

"Who? Gestur?"

"Gestur."

"I see," Neville says.

"So I've let everybody down. You. Grandma. Stephansson. Even your friend Gunnar who translated that poem."

Owen's granddad puts his arm around Owen.

"Listen to me. It was a terrible time. For all of us. Maybe especially for you. Everyone handles grief differently. It can make us do things we don't expect. Things we might never do otherwise."

Owen puts his head in his hands.

"It's true," Neville insists. "Why, I know of a woman back home in Red Deer whose husband died years ago. Tragic, really. Always tinkering. He fell off a ladder while cleaning out their roof gutters. Anyway, she once confessed to me that she talks to her husband as if he were alive, still puttering around the house. It makes her feel less lonely to pretend he's there."

Owen says nothing.

"Poor Marge Figgis," Neville adds.

Owen sits up. He remembers Marge Figgis from his grandmother's funeral. He shakes his head.

"Pops. I don't think I copied because of grief. I think I copied because I thought my poem had to be perfect. I tried, but I couldn't write a perfect poem."

"So now you know. Writing poetry is hard," Neville says. "And you can't expect to be good at everything."

Owen stares at his granddad.

"I thought I *was* good at everything," he says.

"Who told you that?" Neville asks.

"Everyone. 'Owen does this, Owen does that.' You all say it," Owen says.

"Owen. You aren't perfect."

"No?"

"No. Believe me." Neville says, but his voice is kind, even playful.

The words sink in. Owen is surprised that he doesn't feel insulted. Instead, he feels grateful. Grateful and relieved.

Owen lays his head on his granddad's shoulder.

"I'm so sorry."

"Of course you are," Neville says.

They stay on the bench for a bit. Eventually, Owen lifts his head.

"I want to make this right," he announces, plucking his notebook from the ground.

He lays it on his lap and carefully rips out the last page. He folds the poem and stuffs it into his pocket alongside the pen from the archive.

His granddad watches with raised eyebrows as Owen stuffs his imperfect green notebook with the missing page into his knapsack.

Owen has been saving all of his notebooks since first grade, each one in mint condition, a perfect record.

Until now.

Aris returns right on schedule, and she has brought them sandwiches to eat on the way.

They pile into her car and drive. Everyone has grown somber.

"We're getting close to Stephansson's monument now," Aris says with reverence. "This area is where his family first farmed."

Owen peers out his window, his forehead pressing on the fogged glass.

It is so desolate outside. So bleak. He doesn't even spot sheep. There are only bumpy, barren fields of black rocks and green moss. A small brook cuts a path through some rolling foothills among misty patches. Mountains loom in the distance, still capped in snow.

Aris pulls off the road onto a small look-off point. They pile out of the car. Wordlessly, as if at a funeral service, they walk single file along a short footpath, uphill to the top where a national historic monument dedicated to Stephansson has been built. It is tall and made of local stone and concrete shaped like a steeple. There is a carved metal plaque fixed to one side that shows Stephansson composing poems at his Alberta homestead.

Everyone separates to walk around the monument at their own pace, each taking in the spectacularly raw landscape below.

"This must look exactly as it did when Stephansson stood on this very hill," Neville says with awe. "Gunnar would be so pleased to know we made it here."

When no one is looking, Owen takes the poem out of his pocket and unfolds it. Beneath his own name he writes, *Some verses were written by Stephan G. Stephansson, translated by Gunnar Ingvarsson.*

He refolds the poem.

Tight.

He finds a crevice between some of the stones at the base of the monument and tucks the wadded paper deep inside where it will remain protected for as long as Owen can imagine.

He stands up. The bleak surroundings look brighter. The sun is burning through the fog patches. A great weight has been lifted. He catches his granddad's eye and smiles.

Aris glances at her cell phone.

"Oh, look at the time," she says regretfully. "I really must be off. Remember, you'll have about thirty minutes here before my colleagues fetch you for the drive back to Reykjavík. You'll be flying home to Canada in no time."

"Thank you, Aris," Neville says. "For everything."

"My pleasure," Aris says. "It was wonderful to meet you both."

She gives Owen's granddad a hug.

"Come back to the car with me," she says to Owen. "You can help me with the luggage."

Owen follows her down the footpath to the car while his granddad finds a good place to sit at the base of the monument. He quietly contemplates the mountains in the distance, his white tufts of hair lifted by the wind.

Back at the car, Aris opens the trunk. They both lift out the luggage and set it by the start of

THE THINGS OWEN WROTE

the footpath along with Owen's knapsack and his granddad's briefcase.

"Owen," Aris says, turning to him, her face suddenly serious. "I had a phone call last night. Well, rather, your grandfather had a phone call last night, but I answered."

"What do you mean?" Owen asks.

"After I walked him back to your room, I returned to the TV lounge to finish watching the news. When I went to go to bed, I noticed that he had left his cell phone on the coffee table. By then, it was much too late to disturb you both, so I brought it to my room for safekeeping."

Owen tosses the knapsack over his shoulder. He is surprised at how tired he suddenly feels, how heavy his knapsack has become. He is a worn-out traveler who just wants to go home.

"The phone rang in the middle of the night," Aris continues. "I answered it thinking it was my cell. I thought it might have something to do with Britta and I panicked. But the call wasn't for me."

Aris steps closer to Owen to look him in the face.

"It was Marge Figgis," she says.

"Marge Figgis?" Owen repeats.

"Marge Figgis. A friend of your grandfather's. Well, in fact, there were a few ladies with her. She was on speakerphone calling from your grandfather's living room."

Owen feels like he is sinking. He knows who the ladies in the room with her must be. The ladies from the Red Deer River Readers Book Club. His granddad forgot to call them about the casseroles from the airport, Owen now realizes.

"They've been helping out your grandfather with meals and such for some time now. They knew he was taking care of you this week, so they've been dropping off casseroles on your front porch. Only, the food's been piling up at your door. Uneaten. They're worried."

"What did you tell them?" Owen asks.

"They wanted to know who I was and where you and your grandfather were," Aris says. "They wanted to be sure you're okay."

"Me? I'm fine."

"Still. They're worried about you. They ..." Aris stops. She sighs.

"They what?" Owen asks.

"They insisted on calling your parents."

"Oh," Owen says.

Owen looks away.

"Do your parents know that you're in Iceland?" Aris asks gently.

"Yes," Owen says, glancing at Aris. "Pops called them."

But Owen isn't so sure now.

After a few seconds, Owen adds truthfully, "Or maybe he forgot."

Aris nods.

They both turn to the hillock with the tall monument that looks like a steeple. Owen's granddad is still sitting, still admiring the view, his back to them.

"They insisted on calling your parents," Aris repeats. "So I went down to the front desk and looked up the phone number you wrote on the register. "I ..." she pauses again. "I gave it to them."

Owen realizes that he did not write his home telephone number on the register. Out of habit, he wrote down the number that he calls the most.

"My mom's cell phone," Owen concludes. "She'll have that with her in Las Vegas."

He sets down his knapsack on the dusty path in defeat.

"I'm so sorry, Owen. I didn't want to get your grandfather into trouble. I like him very much. But ..."

Aris's voice trails.

"But what?" Owen asks, dreading the awful truth.

"But they claim that he has been displaying unpredictable behavior over the past few months. He's also becoming forgetful. It's something your parents need to know about."

In that moment, Owen replays all of his grand-dad's slipups in rapid succession.

The confusion on the airplane.

The missing driver's license.

The muddle with the cutlery.

The suitcase full of socks.

"Listen," she says kindly. "There's a six-hour time-zone difference between Iceland and Alberta, seven hours for Las Vegas. Marge said they'd wait until the morning to call your parents."

Aris pulls out the cell phone that belongs to Owen's granddad from her bag and checks the charge on it before handing it to Owen.

"I expect they'll call within the hour. I'm telling you now so that you can prepare, so that you can be there for your grandfather."

Owen reluctantly takes the cell phone.

"I have to go," Aris says apologetically.

She stands awkwardly holding her car keys. They glint in a shaft of Arctic sun.

Owen manages to give the smallest of nods.

Aris takes a step and hugs Owen. Owen hesitates a few seconds, then hugs her back.

"*Þetta reddast*," Aris whispers, kissing him on the cheek.

She climbs into the car and gives a wistful little wave before shutting her door. Owen watches her go until he can no longer see her car. He is surrounded by their luggage with his knapsack at his feet, his granddad's cell phone heavy in his hand.

He turns back to the cold gray monument. All around is forlorn and abandoned farmland. But there is something about Owen's granddad, something about how he is now sitting while taking in the view that is not in keeping with his bleak and gloomy surroundings.

What is he thinking?

Owen sets the cell phone down — the cell phone that is certain to ring any minute — and silently reaches for his camera. He points it at his granddad and uses the lens to zoom in. His granddad turns his head ever so slightly, just enough that Owen sees his profile. His granddad is smiling as if he is at peace with himself, as if he has just accomplished his greatest mission, his greatest triumph.

Owen wants more than anything to record this moment. He steadies his breath while peering through his lens. He does not rush. This time, he waits, knowing he is risking the moment, but he's determined to take that chance. The sun burns through another fog patch. The light improves. Owen slowly pushes the button. The shutter opens for a split second and records everything.

It is the best photograph of his granddad that Owen will ever take.

ELEVEN

MY HEART
by Owen Sharpe

My grandma jogged in bright red running shoes.
She loved to breathe the early-morning air.
Her rhubarb crisp once made the evening news,
when she placed first at Red Deer's county fair.

One time, my granddad rented her a boat;
the parts of it and sailing terms he taught her.
But she said no, she'd really rather float,
and overboard she jumped into the water.

My attic room she painted mossy green;
from there she read to me in bed each night.
She tucked me into sheets so crisp and clean.
Outside the stars would shine so true and bright.

Together we bought jars of fish-food flakes,
a glass bowl and a pretty goldfish, too,
whose brilliant color sings, and my heart aches
to see her shimmering carrot-orange hue.

My grandma showed how tough it was to fight
when she got sick and tired of facing cancer.
She took it all with dignity and might
and the hidden strength of a ballet dancer.

And we who grieve are reconciled to see
that vengeance for her loss can be forsaken,
that goodness had no fault to find with she
and had no cause for her for being taken.

Red Deer's river now slides by so silently,
past rows of markers where my grandma sleeps.
And my empty attic room stands valiantly
where my broken heart is locked inside for keeps.

Her honest kindness cannot ever fade,
will be as years go by my guide and treasure,
though hope has gone for any plans we made
yet I've this gift she gave in generous measure.

GESTUR
by Stephan G. Stephansson
Translated by Paul Sigurdson

The law which cuts life's thinly ravelled thread,
Gave little time for dread or hope or sadness.
It flung a bolt from heaven overhead
And felled my cherished son in its blind madness.
Yet 'tis some comfort, since it had to be,
It caused no previous suffering to me.

And it's some comfort and some good to know,
It was a senseless force that made your ending,
No willful evil thing that struck you so,
But accident, its random strike descending.
It is man's cruelty, where'er it be,
Which cuts the heart with keenest agony.

And those who grieve are reconciled to see
That vengeance for this loss can be forsaken,
That goodness had no fault to find with thee
And had no cause for you for being taken,
For it could never be so mean and cold
To those who mourn your passing from the fold.

And evil cannot rule the good and right.
It matters not what life and death are boding;
It cannot touch you for it lacks the might.
The shaft of lightning from the sky exploding
Was innocent of any willful wrath
As even you who happened in its path.

So now I sing for you my poignant lay
On phrases sweetly blending with my sadness.
Among the blessed angels you will stay,
Forever comforted by joy and gladness.
And thus consoled I soothe the grief that sears,
And bless your name 'mid thankfulness and tears.

I am consoled, but yet I feel the pain
For those who grieve their every hour waking,
That I can bear no fragment of their strain
When I the greater part should now be taking,
But you'll be with me 'til life's ending day,
Blent with my every task, my every day.

Your honest kindness cannot ever fade,
Will be as years go by my guide and treasure,
Though hope has gone for any plans we made
Yet I've this gift you gave in generous measure.
When my last song is sung and I find rest
Life will keep kindness in its tender breast.

Oh dearest child! A cheerful willing boy,
A strength to guide and help me in my ageing,
That in my weariness I'd find some joy,
In recomposing half-forgotten pages.
But I'd forsake that gift with joyous tears,
If I could grant you life for added years.

You'll be remembered in my sweetest lays,
Until the sun has dimmed my golden hours,
Until the world has turned my final days,
Until your grave is overgrown with flowers,
And hallowed to thy grave my way shall be
As my last poem to your memory.

STEPHAN G. STEPHANSSON

Stephan was an Icelandic Canadian poet, often referred to as the Poet of the Rocky Mountains. He was self-educated and worked as a farmer all his life, providing for his wife and eight children. Eventually, he settled in Alberta where, being an insomniac, he often wrote till dawn after farming all day. Stephansson wrote only in Icelandic, leaving his work to the skills of his translators. He is considered by Iceland to be one of their best poets since the thirteenth century. His literary topics included the immigrant experience, landscape, community, human ambition and progress, and equal rights for men and women.

Stephan G. Stephansson was born Stefán Guðmundur Guðmundsson on October 3, 1853, in the Skagafjörður district of North Iceland, and died on August 10, 1927, near Markerville, Alberta. His homestead near Markerville is now an Alberta Provincial Historic Site and has been open to the public since 1982.

THE ORDER OF THE FALCON

The president of Iceland presents the Order of the Falcon to worthy individuals twice each year. The

Order of the Falcon harkens back to the Icelandic Vikings, who gave two traditional gifts to exceptional people they met on their travels: poetry and live Icelandic falcons. Today, the medal is given in gratitude on behalf of the people of Iceland to those who demonstrate dedication, loyalty and leadership in preserving Icelandic culture. The medal is retained during the recipient's lifetime, but it is supposed to be returned to the Icelandic government upon his or her death. Stephansson's wife, Helga Sigríður Jónsdóttir, was awarded the medal in recognition of her distinguished husband after Stephansson died. Helga died in 1940. The whereabouts of her medal are unknown.

ACKNOWLEDGMENTS

When I lived in Alberta and studied at the University of Calgary, I spent a summer working for what was then called Alberta Historic Sites Services as an interpreter. I was assigned to a new site called Stephansson House Provincial Historic Site near Markerville. We opened the house each day and wore 1920s period clothing in keeping with the decade that Stephansson died.

I spent countless hours in the poet-farmer's homestead, surrounded by his belongings, whiling away the hours between visitors by attempting to grow a garden or spinning wool. I didn't get very good at either.

Three things stayed with me over the years. Stephansson's attic had become home to an enormous bat colony. We could hear and smell them through the walls. Occasionally, one would escape and make its way into the living quarters, and I would discover it when I opened the house in the morning. It was disconcerting.

The second was the tragic way in which Stephansson's son Gestur died. Who could forget that story and the moving poem that accompanied it? The ghostly photograph of the boy and his nearby grave marker haunted me as I stared out over the prairies where he lay.

The third was the contradiction between Stephansson's fame in Iceland and his relative obscurity in Canada, owing to the fact that he wrote all his work in Icelandic. I now appreciate how important literary translators are in championing work to new audiences, as well as archivists who keep meticulous records of the past for us to discover. I worked with both during the research of this novel.

In Canada, thank you to Lindsay Ballagray, Red Deer and District Archives; Brooke Henrikson and Marlene Linneberg, Stephan G. Stephansson Icelandic Society; Angie Friesen, Provincial Archives of Alberta; Olga Fowler, Historic Sites and Museums, Alberta Culture and Tourism; Alexa Murray, Stephansson House; and Chelsea Butler, Historic Markerville Creamery Museum. Thank you to the Sigurdson family, and in particular to Ivadell Sigurdson for granting permission to reprint the translated poem called "Gestur" by her late husband, Paul Sigurdson. Thank you, too, to Richard Chase, my book-tour coordinator in Lethbridge, Alberta, who told me about how a clump of trees on the prairies likely means that a former homestead once stood there.

In Iceland, I would like to thank the following: Unnar Ingvarsson, National and University Library; Sólborg Una Pálsdóttirr, Skagafjörður Archive; Lára Ágústa Ólafsdóttir, District Archives of Akureyi; Snorri Guðjón Sigurðsson, District Archives of Þingeyjarsýsla; Bragi Þorgrímur Ólafsson, National Museum of Iceland and National Archives; Valgeir Thorvaldsson, Icelandic Emigration Centre at Hofsós; and the President's Office of Protocol.

I would also like to acknowledge three books that I pored over as part of my research: *Wakeful Nights* by Viðar Hreinsson; *Stephan G. Stephansson: Selected translations from Andvökur* by the Stephan G. Stephansson Homestead Restoration Committee; and *Stephan G. Stephansson: Selected Prose & Poetry*, translated by Kristjana Gunnars. If you are interested in learning more about this great poet, these are excellent sources.

My firsthand research in Iceland was made possible by a grant from the Access Copyright Foundation, for which I am deeply grateful. I am also grateful to my husband, Peter, to whom I read several early drafts, and who drove me around the Ring Road in Iceland to support my research. Finally, I am indebted to Sheila Barry at Groundwood Books for her many candid insights, which helped me wrestle this manuscript to the ground, and to Emma Sakamoto for her copy-editing expertise.

Neville Sharpe was created after a conversation I had with my son, who at the time was a volunteer at the Camp Hill Veterans Memorial hospital in Halifax. Elliott told me about a very nice elderly man who struggled because he had no short-term memory. He didn't know where he was, from one minute to the next. All he could remember was his career as a butcher and his wife of long ago. He kept telling Elliott that he wanted to go home, and Elliott would have to patiently explain, yet again, why he was living at the hospital for good. The elderly man would listen carefully, and having learned of his situation as if for the first time, would then ask the same question.

"So, what do I do now?"

Heartbreaking.

Standing alongside Stephansson's monument on the northern coast in Iceland, I knew that I would use this historic hillock in the last scene of my novel. Both Owen and his granddad would be at peace in this place, this final destination. But what, I wondered, would Stephan G. Stephansson and Owen's grandmother Aileen Sharpe say, having learned about the things Owen wrote? Would they forgive Owen? If they had also been standing on this very hillock, here's how I think that conversation might go.

EXT. SITE OF STEPHANSSON'S MONUMENT IN NORTHERN ICELAND — DAY

Owen's grandmother AILEEN SHARPE is jogging in red running shoes along the Ring Road of Iceland toward the Stephan G. Stephansson historic monument perched atop a small hillock. The sun is high and the morning's fog patches are burning off. There is no traffic.

She spots a man up ahead near a swift brook that runs behind the hillock. He is plucking up, then discarding, small objects from the ground.

Aileen detours off the road and picks her way through the moss-dressed rocky field until she reaches the man who is bent down at the brook. He does not spot her at first, so lost in his task while reciting a poem out loud to himself.

MAN
How deeply I love you, heath of my fathers, / covered with birch bushes, sparkling with streams. / The swans on your waters sing every morning, / building their nests on the ruins of farms.

The man turns to look at Aileen. It is STEPHAN G. STEPHANSSON, an Icelandic poet. He is thin and wiry, with black hair, full mustache and ice-blue eyes. He's cleanly dressed as if he is between stops on a book tour.

> **AILEEN**
> (out of breath)
> I thought I recognized you from the old photographs! You're Stephan G. Stephansson!

> **STEPHAN**
> (delighted)
> I am. And you are?

> **AILEEN**
> Aileen Sharpe. So nice to meet you!

They shake hands. She unstraps her empty water bottle from her belt, steps to the edge of the brook and begins to fill it.

> **AILEEN (CONT'D)**
> Gunnar's right. Iceland is beautiful.

> **STEPHAN**
> (peering past her down the road)

Gunnar Ingvarsson? My Alberta translator?
Is he with you?

AILEEN
No. We traveled to Iceland together, but
after shopping for an itchy Nordic sweater, I
left him at the archive. Now he's knee-deep
in your letters.

STEPHAN
Well, he is my biggest fan.

AILEEN
(taking a drink of her water)
This glacial water is delicious. Want a sip?

STEPHAN
No, thanks.

AILEEN
So, what are you doing here?

STEPHAN
I like to come back from time to time. My
old family horse was buried here, somewhere along this creek.

AILEEN

Oh?

STEPHAN

That was so long ago. Even the stone cairn
I built to honor him is gone. I loved that
horse. We named him Skór. It means shoes.
He had a white hoof.

AILEEN

Fond memories.

STEPHAN

Yes, fond memories. I tried to capture as
many as I could in my poems.

AILEEN

As did my grandson, Owen. He tried at any
rate.

STEPHAN

Ah, yes. Owen. What a shame. But then,
we've all done things we're ashamed about,
haven't we?

AILEEN

True. I'm ashamed of how badly I behaved when Neville rented that sailboat on our honeymoon. I'm sorry I never did apologize to him for that.

STEPHAN

But Owen has apologized, which I accept.

AILEEN

You're very understanding.

STEPHAN

As I said, we've all done things for which we're not proud.

AILEEN

Even an accomplished poet like you?

STEPHAN

Of course. I've had plenty of shameful moments. There's one moment in particular that this place reminds me about.

AILEEN

Oh? What happened?

STEPHAN

(after a beat)

Back when I lived here as a child in the 1850s, I was out in this very field, minding our small flock of sheep. It was a cool day, the winds were biting, but it was not yet winter. My mother was at home, tending to my younger sister who was sick in bed. My father was away getting supplies.

AILEEN

Were you worried to be on your own in such a remote place?

STEPHAN

Not particularly. Actually, I had a book with me and found a place to read behind this hillock and out of the wind but where I could still watch the sheep. I settled in and was quite content with having time to myself. Then, at some point, I heard voices.

AILEEN

Voices? From ghosts?

STEPHAN

No, real voices. Voices that carried in the
wind. I got up and climbed to the top of this
hillock to have a better look. That's when
I spotted them. Three neighbor farm boys
walking on their long journey south to
Reykjavík.

AILEEN

Why were they going to Reykjavík?

STEPHAN

That's what I wanted to know. When I asked,
they told me they were going to school. To
learn. They told me about the teachers, the
books, the classes. They were thrilled. They
even invited me to come with them.

AILEEN

You wanted to go, didn't you?

STEPHAN

Desperately. More than anything. But I
knew I couldn't. I had one book in my hand
and a few more back home, but that was it.

AILEEN

Your family had no money.

STEPHAN

No money for school at any rate. We could barely pay our rent to the church that owned our croft.

AILEEN

So what happened?

STEPHAN

The boys wished me well and left me standing atop this barren windy hillock. All I could do was watch them until they disappeared from my view. One minute I'm lost in my book. The next minute I'm absolutely and inconsolably heartbroken. I think I wanted to die. I curled up in the lee of this hillock and wept. I wept for hours.

AILEEN

Such a bitter disappointment.

STEPHAN

That wasn't the worst of it. My mother came out to search for me. She was terribly worried. As soon as she found me, I quickly dried my eyes, but I knew from my mother's expression that she knew. She could see my disappointment, my tear-streaked face.

AILEEN

She believed she was to blame for your situation, your bad fortune.

STEPHAN

That's right. But my parents couldn't help their lot. I knew that they were doing their best for me. They were not to blame.

AILEEN

No. They were doing their best, as you say.

Stephan pauses to stare up at his monument. He clears his throat.

STEPHAN (CONT'D)

My mother was devastated. And I was the cause of her devastation, not our family's poverty. It was that shameful unspoken moment between us that I shall never forget.

Stephan continues to stare past Aileen toward his monument.

STEPHAN (CONT'D)
On the day we left Iceland for North America, I vowed to myself that I would become a great poet, even if I had to farm every day for the rest of my life. I would make my mother proud. And so I became the farmer-poet of the Rockies.

AILEEN
All because of what happened on this windy hillock.

STEPHAN
Yes. Decades later, I was finally invited back to Iceland for a book tour. I traveled from Reykjavík all the way up the northern coast, visiting villages along the way until I came here, to where we first farmed. We stopped for the night. In the morning, I got up early and took a long walk on my own.
(smiling)
Even back then, our croft was in ruins, but I found this very hillock.

AILEEN

How did that make you feel? Coming home
after all those years?

STEPHAN

In a word, triumphant. Like a little fish who
crossed a great big pond and somehow
made it back.

Stephan extends his hand to Aileen and opens his
palm.

STEPHAN (CONT'D)

Look what I found.

He drops a large but twisted and heavily corroded
iron nail into her hand. She studies it.

STEPHAN (CONT'D)

It's from the Viking era.

AILEEN

Holy smokes. What a remarkable find!

STEPHAN

Not really. This land has been occupied for
over a thousand years. Nails like this are

more common than you'd think. They're often found among the collapsed turf walls of Viking longhouses.

Aileen hands the nail back to Stephan. He digs a small hole in the ground, drops the nail in and buries it. He stands, wiping his hands on his pants.

Aileen takes a long drink of water from her bottle and as she does, she turns away from Stephan to look up at his monument. He looks up at the monument, too.

> **AILEEN**
> It's an impressive tribute.

> **STEPHAN**
> (sighing)
> There's a typo on my plaque.

> **AILEEN**
> (turning to face Stephan, shocked)
> No!

> **STEPHAN**
> (pained)
> And some punctuation errors, as well.

AILEEN
(hand on chest)
Ouch!

She bends to tie a shoelace that has come undone.

STEPHAN
(whispering)
We have visitors.

AILEEN
(standing up, following his gaze to the
monument, her voice cracking)
Those are my boys. Neville and Owen. I
miss them so.

She hugs herself as if suddenly chilled by the distant snow-capped mountains. She watches as Owen digs out his camera and takes a photograph of his granddad, his granddad unaware that his portrait is being taken.

They are both looking her way.

STEPHAN
(softly)
How poetic. If only they could see you.

Aileen doesn't answer. Instead, she takes a bold step toward Neville and Owen, and blows two heartfelt kisses that carry to them in the wind.

FADE TO BLACK.